Brand of Outlaws

A Western Novel

Ken Cannon

Shadowplay Communications, LLC

Copyright © 2023 by Ken Cannon

All rights reserved.

No portion of this book may be reproduced in any form without written permission from the publisher or author, except as permitted by U.S. copyright law.

Contents

1. Chapter One.   1
2. Chapter Two.   21
3. Chapter Three.   41
4. Chapter Four.   64
5. Chapter Five.   81
6. Chapter Six.   104
7. Chapter Seven.   116
8. Chapter Eight.   135
9. Chapter Nine.   148
10. Chapter Ten.   156
11. Chapter Eleven.   173
12. Chapter Twelve.   191
13. Chapter Thirteen.   202
14. Chapter Fourteen.   217
15. Chapter Fifteen.   227

Chapter One.

After an early breakfast, I took a stroll up and down the main street of Sanderson, gathering information and making observations that could come in handy later. I returned to the hotel, ready for whatever the day had in store. As I approached, I noticed a stage-coach already packed with passengers, but it wasn't heading to Linrock. However, I had discovered that another stage left for that destination three times a week. I spotted several cowboy broncos tied to a railing, and a bit further down the road, two buckboards with horses that caught my attention. These had to be the teams that Colonel Barkley had mentioned to Reuben Darling. Just then, both men emerged from the hotel, and Darling noticed me. He signaled Barkley before walking over to me.

"Are you Tim, the cowboy?" he asked.

I nodded and sized him up. In the daylight, he was just as impressive as he had been in the evening, but the light didn't do much for his dark complexion.

"Here's your pay," he said, handing me some bills. "Miss Barkley doesn't need your services at the ranch anymore."

"What do you mean? This is the first I'm hearing of it," I replied.

"Sorry, kid. That's all there is to it," he said, cutting me off. "She gave me the money and told me to pay you off. You don't need to speak to her about it."

In other words, he was saying that even a goodbye with Miss Barkley was not desirable. As luck would have it, the girls appeared at that moment, and I went straight to them. I was relieved that Reuben Darling couldn't help but notice the warm welcome I received from Miss Barkley. Her smile and "Good morning, Tim" showed no sign that I was not to continue serving her indefinitely. As I had expected, she had no idea that Darling had fired me on her behalf.

"Miss Barkley," I said, dismayed. "What have I done?"

"Why'd you let me go?" She looked shocked. "Tim, I don't get it."

"Why'd you fire me?" I pressed on, trying to look devastated. "I haven't even had a chance yet. I really wanted to work for you, Miss Gwen. What did I do wrong? Why'd you let me go?"

"I didn't," Miss Barkley stated firmly, her dark eyes sparkling. "But hold on, here's my pay," I continued, showing her the money. "Mr. Darling just came up to me and said you sent this over, that you wouldn't need me at the ranch anymore."

Miss Gwen let out a little gasp. She seemed taken aback by what she had heard. "My cousin Reuben said that?" she asked me.

I nodded my head vigorously. At that moment, Darling walked up to us, practically shoving me aside. "Come on, ladies, let's take a walk before we leave," he said cheerfully. "I'll show you Sanderson."

"Wait, please," Miss Barkley interjected, looking directly at him. "Cousin Reuben, I think there's a mistake, maybe a misunderstanding. This is the cowboy I hired, Mr. Tim. He says you gave him money and told him I fired him."

"Yes, cousin, I did," he retorted, his voice getting louder. A hint of red crept up his cheeks. "We don't need him at the ranch. We have plenty of other boys. I just wanted to let him down easy and not bother you."

It was clear that Reuben Darling had made a grave error. First, Miss Barkley was utterly bewildered, then disappointed, and finally, she lifted her head with a sort of haughty elegance. She would have addressed him directly, but Colonel Barkley approached us. "Dad, did you tell Reuben to fire Tim?" she asked him.

"I definitely did not," the colonel replied with a chuckle. "Reuben acted on his own."

"Is that so? I'd like my cousin to understand that I'm my own boss. I've always taken care of my own affairs, and I'll keep doing so. Tim, I'm sorry you've been treated this way."

"Listen up, from now on you take orders from me," Colonel Barkley barked at me. "So, does that mean I'm going to Linrock with you?" I asked. "Of course. Ride with Gwen and me today," he replied. As they walked away, I noticed Darling's discomfort.

Colonel Barkley seemed to relish it. "Diane's just like her mother," he said to Reuben. "You've made a terrible first impression." Darling's temper flared up, and I could tell he was a dangerous man. "Tim, let me tell you," he said, leaning in close to me. "Don't go to Linrock." "Hey, Mr. Darling," I blustered, trying to sound tough. "If you threaten me, I'll have you thrown in jail!" Both men were taken aback by my response. Darling was at a loss for words. "Are you really going to Linrock?" he asked, his voice thick with anger. I looked at him differently than I had before. "You bet I am," I replied with a caustic tone. Colonel Barkley intervened, grabbing Darling's arm. They both looked at me with interest. I walked away, not bothering to listen to their conversation. "Reuben, your temper will get you in trouble one day," Colonel Barkley warned. "You'll mess with the wrong guy eventually. Look, here come Joe and Brick!" I turned my attention to the two cowboys. One had fiery red hair and the other had a bold demeanor. They were the type of cowboys the Rangers called four-flushes, hard-drinking, devil-may-care types who packed guns and were always looking for trouble. Although the Rangers had a high standard for bravery, cowboys like these could still be dangerous to ordinary men. The smaller of the two was Joe, and when Darling spoke to him, he turned to look at me, his thin mouth slanting down in a menacing way.

Brick gave me a once-over, and I could tell he wasn't a seasoned cowboy. Right off the bat, I had three adversaries: Darling and his crew. But honestly, I would have butted heads with them no matter what. I had a feeling that we were on the verge of a confrontation, but Miss Barkley interrupted my thoughts by calling out to me.

"Get our bags, Tim," she said. I quickly grabbed them and saw that Darling and his posse had already saddled up. Colonel Barkley was in the lead buckboard with two unfamiliar men, while the girls rode in the second one. The driver of the second buckboard was a tall, skinny teenager who looked like he was still growing. We were all cramped for space, but that wasn't going to ruin the ride for me.

We followed the leaders through the town's main street and out onto a well-worn road that stretched northwest. To our left were the bleak mountains I had noticed yesterday, and to our right was a flat, mesquite-covered expanse. The driver urged his horses into a fast trot, and we kept close to Colonel Barkley who was having an intense conversation with his companions.

The girls behind me were losing interest in the ride as we approached our destination of Linrock. They chatted about what the town might be like, while I occasionally asked the driver some questions. Unfortunately, the ride wasn't as exciting as it was yesterday. Every half-mile or so, we passed a ranch house, and as we got further out from Sanderson, the ranches became few and far between. Eventually, they were so spread out that each one stood alone in the vast wilderness.

As we rode along, we came across a stream that flowed north. I was surprised to see the amount of water it carried. It must have come from the mountains far west. The sandy ground was covered in tufts of grass, but it was so high and thick that it could easily graze a million head of stock, considering the immense area in sight. In the forenoon, we made three stops. The first was at a suitable place to water the horses, the second was at a chuckwagon belonging to cowboys who were out riding after stock, and the third was at a small cluster of adobe and stone houses constituting a hamlet the driver called Barkley, named after the Colonel. From that point on to Linrock, there were only a few ranches, each one controlling great acreage.

Early in the afternoon, we sighted Linrock from a ridgetop. It was a green path amidst the mass of gray. For the barrens of Texas, it was indeed a fair sight. But I was more concerned about its remoteness from civilization than its beauty. In the early 1870s, when the vast western third of Texas was a wilderness, the pioneer had done wonders to settle there and establish places like Linrock. As we rolled swiftly along, the whole sweeping range was dotted with cattle, and farther on, within a few miles of town, there were droves of horses that brought enthusiastic praise from Miss Barkley and her cousin.

"There's plenty of room here for long rides," I said, waving my hand at the gray-green expanse. "Your horses won't suffer on this range." She was delighted, and her cousin, for once, seemed speechless. "That's the ranch," said the driver, pointing with his whip. It only took a glance for me to see that Colonel Barkley's ranch was on a scale fitting the country. The house was situated on the only elevation around Linrock, and it was not high, nor more than a few minutes' walk from the edge of town.

The structure before us was a sprawling, flat-roofed building made of red adobe bricks that seemed to cover an entire acre of land. Everything was lush and green, except for the corrals and barns that were fenced off and painted in shades of gray and red. As we approached, Darling and the cowboys vanished into the cottonwood trees, leaving Colonel Barkley waiting for us beside the buckboard. His expression was the best I had seen on him thus far, radiating warmth, love, and a hint of melancholy. His daughter was equally agitated, and I quickly offered my seat to the Colonel, sensing that this was not the time for me to be in the spotlight.

I took advantage of the situation and turned towards the town, walking leisurely through the shady outskirts of Linrock. My feelings were a mix of curiosity, eagerness, and anticipation as I strolled down a side street, passing small red houses nestled among oak and cottonwood trees. I walked all the way to the other end of the street, crossing several intersections, encountering children, well-dressed women, and dusty-booted men. I turned right at a right angle and headed up several blocks until I reached a tree-lined plaza. On the other side of the plaza was a broad street that, despite the number of horses and people, had a sleepy air about it. I remained alert, taking in everything around me, wondering if I would run into Foster and how I would recognize him. But I felt confident that I could spot the Ranger out of a thousand strangers, even though we had never met.

As I continued walking, the residences gave way to buildings that fronted right onto the stone sidewalk. I passed a grain store, a hardware store, and a grocery store, and then several empty buildings and a vacant corner.

The following block, apart from the rough exteriors of the crude structures, would have been considered a small town in eastern Texas. Evidence of business consistent with a prosperous community of two thousand inhabitants was visible. On both sides of the street, the next block was a solid row of saloons, resorts, and hotels. There were saddled horses hitched along the sidewalk in two long lines, with a buckboard and team here and there breaking the continuity. This block was bustling and noisy. From all appearances, Linrock was like any other frontier town, and my expectations were barely met.

As the afternoon was coming to a close, I retraced my steps and went back to the ranch. The driver boy, whom I had heard called Dick, was looking for me, apparently at Miss Barkley's request, and he led me to the house. It was even more massive than I had imagined from a distance, and the adobe bricks were worn smooth by rain and wind. As we walked by, I got a glimpse in at several doors. There was comfort here that spoke volumes about the many freighter's trips from Del Rio. I was pleased to see things that were little short of luxurious for that part of the country, for the sake of the young ladies.

At the far end of the house, Dick took me to a small room that was very satisfactory to me. I asked about bunkhouses for the cowboys, and he said they were full to overflowing. "Colonel Barkley has a big outfit, huh?" "I reckon he does," replied Dick. "I don't know how many cowboys there are. They're always coming and going. I'm not acquainted with half of them." "Is there a lot of stock movement these days?" "Stock's always moving," he replied with a strange look. "Rustlers?" But he didn't follow up with the affirmative I expected. "Linrock is a lively place, I hear?" "It's not as lively as Sanderson, but it's bigger." "Yes, I heard it was."

I overheard a conversation about two cowboys who were recently arrested. I asked about it and was told that they were Joe Bean and Brick Higgins, who belonged to the ranch but were not often around. Not wanting to seem too curious, I changed the subject. It turned out that Miss Barkley, whom I was working for, had not left any instructions for me, so I had supper with Dick in the kitchen. He told me that the cowboys cooked their own meals at their bunks, and assumed that I would eat at the ranch-house. After supper, I explored the ranch and was impressed with the horses and the overall beauty of the place. I saw Miss Barkley and her cousin approaching with their dog, but avoided them. As the sun set, I headed into town to find Foster, but I had to be discreet about it. I walked up and down the main street until it got dark, then went into a hotel and later a rough-looking establishment that was surprisingly nice inside. The place was crowded with dusty cowboys, and I listened to their conversations while I sat and watched. I eventually found a saloon where most of the patrons had been or were going, and it was a large room with a bar and many tables and chairs.

This had to be the gambling establishment mentioned in the Ranger's letter to Captain Neal and the one rumored to be owned by the Linrock mayor. It was the only sizable gambling spot in southern Texas where I'd observed the absence of Mexicans. There was some card playing happening when I arrived. I lingered for a bit, aware that strangers were too common in Linrock to draw attention. However, I couldn't spot anyone who resembled Foster. I left, feeling a little defeated. It had always been a point of pride for me that I couldn't spend an hour in an unfamiliar town or walk down a dimly lit street without experiencing something out of the ordinary. Some people called it luck, but I knew it was because I was always on the lookout for adventure. Nevertheless, on my first day and night in Linrock, despite my watchfulness and curiosity, it seemed that I was in for a disappointment. I was thinking this when I arrived at the last lit-up place on the block, a shabby little restaurant. Just then, a tall, dark figure passed by me and disappeared into the darkness. There was a man sitting on the low steps, and another standing in the doorway. "That was the guy everyone in town is talking about, the Ranger," said one man. I froze in the shadows, where I couldn't be seen. "Really? Is he staying here?" asked the other. "Yep," answered the man called Jim, emitting a humorless laugh. "He's been all my business lately. And he's offered to rent my old adobe house just outside town, you know, where I used to live before moving here. He's coming to look at it tomorrow." "Good Lord! Does he expect to stay?" "Seems so."

"He's a real tough guy, that one. He's calm and collected, but there's something about him that just screams danger," said Jim.

"Ah, Jim, he can't hang around here. He's just looking for someone," replied the other man.

"I don't know what his plan is, but he's been here for a while and he's made an impression on me. Just now he asked me where Barkley lives. I asked him if he was going to pay a visit to our mayor, and he said yes. So I gave him directions to the ranch and he headed out that way," explained Jim.

"The hell he did!" exclaimed the other man.

I gathered from the man's reaction that he was both amazed and amused. Then the two men went into the restaurant and I decided to introduce myself to the owner. The most important thing was that I had found Foster. I hurried ahead, thinking he had walked quickly. I reached the plaza, crossed it, and then wasn't sure which direction to take. But I didn't think it mattered, so I just hurried on, hoping to reach the ranch before Foster did. I wasn't sure if I had succeeded, but the moon was bright and I could hear a cowboy singing in the distance. There wasn't a soul in sight on the porch or in the courtyard. I didn't know what the inside of the house looked like, but when I peeked in the first window, I saw a large room where Miss Barkley and Gwen were sitting alone. It was a cozy room with white walls, a fireplace, and a big table with books and papers on it.

Slowly backing away, I noticed that the room had a door leading out to the porch and two more windows. I listened, hoping to hear Foster's footsteps making their way up the road. But all I heard was Gwen's laughter and her cousin's soothing voice. Then, in the distance, I spotted some lit windows at the other end of the front part of the house. I made my way down there and found an open door. Through it, I saw a room that looked exactly like the one I had just left. Inside were Colonel Barkley, Darling, and a few other men, all of them smoking and chatting. It might have been interesting to stick around and listen, but I had to get back to the road to catch Foster.

I quickly retraced my steps and sat down on the porch steps. Then, out of the corner of my eye, I saw a very tall, dark figure approaching in the moonlit road. It was Foster! I wanted to shout out in excitement like a little boy. He came towards me slowly, looking all around, and then stopped about twenty paces away. He surveyed the house, and then, spotting me, started coming forward again. At first, I was struck by how big he was, but then I noticed that his face was hidden in the shadow of his sombrero. I had planned to reveal my identity as soon as I saw him, but I hesitated. He was affecting me in a strange way, or maybe it was just the realization that we Rangers, who had so much in common and so much at stake, had finally come face to face.

"Is Barkley at home?" he asked abruptly.

"Yes," I replied.

"Ask him if he'll see Vaughn Foster, Ranger."

"Wait here," I said. I didn't want to waste any time explaining why I was there. I made a deliberate show of striding down the porch and entering the room where the men were smoking. I walked farther than I needed to just to announce my errand. I wanted to see Barkley's face, to look into his eyes. When I entered, the talking stopped, and I saw nothing but his face, which looked blank.

"Vaughn Foster, Ranger, come to see you, sir," I said.

Did Barkley flinch or show any sign of surprise when I made my announcement? It was hard to say for sure, but there was definitely a change in him. Darling, on the other hand, let out a sharp breath that sounded more like certainty than surprise. Barkley motioned for silence and I knew he was in charge.

"Did Foster say why he wanted to see me?" Barkley asked me.

"No, sir," I replied.

"Tell him I'm not home, Tim," Barkley ordered as he relit his pipe.

As I left the room, I could feel the gears in my mind starting to turn. I knew there was more to this than Barkley was letting on.

"Mr. Foster," I said as I approached him, "Colonel Barkley says he's not at home. You can tell your business to his daughter."

Without waiting for a response, I knocked on the parlor door. Miss Barkley answered, dressed in white and looking as lovely as ever.

"Miss Barkley, here is Vaughn Foster to see you," I said.

"Please come in," she said graciously.

Foster had to duck his head to enter the room. He was an imposing figure, with a stern, chiseled face and piercing eyes. He wore a gray flannel shirt, corduroys, and a big gun on his hip.

I followed him into the room, feeling like an intruder. Miss Barkley didn't seem to mind, though. She was a gracious hostess, and I couldn't help but wonder if Foster's well-known indifference to women would be put to the test in her presence.

I had never seen a Texan as impressive as him before. It wasn't just his towering height or striking features that caught my attention, but something deeper, more spiritual. "Nice to meet you, Mr. Foster," said Miss Barkley, introducing us to her cousin Gwen Langdon. "We just arrived. I'm here to make this my home, and she's visiting me." Foster greeted Gwen with a smile and a bow. He was at ease, with a rough sort of grace, and didn't seem fazed by the presence of two beautiful women. "We've heard of you in Austin," said Gwen, her eyes misbehaving. I hoped I wouldn't have to be jealous of Foster, but this girl seemed like a bit of a flirt. "I didn't expect to be received by ladies," replied Foster. "I came to see Mr. Barkley, but he wouldn't see me. He told me to tell my business to his daughter. I'm glad to know you both, but sorry you've come to Linrock. It's pretty rough around here, not a place for girls to walk and ride." "Why's that?" asked both girls in unison. "Because it's a rough place, and my business has to do with rough characters," said Foster. "Your Ranger duty, right?" asked Miss Barkley. "That's part of it," said Foster. "But my job is to make Linrock a better place." "That's a splendid and worthy task," said Miss Barkley warmly. "I wish you success."

"Mr. Foster, are you saying that Linrock is truly as wicked as you claim?" I asked, my tone incredulous.

"I'm afraid so," he replied firmly.

I could see the doubt in Miss Barkley's eyes as she asked, "And my father refused to see you? Did he not want to cooperate?"

"That's correct," Foster confirmed.

"Please, Mr. Foster, tell me what is happening in Linrock and what it is that you are supposed to do," she implored, her expression serious. "I know my father considers himself the law there. Perhaps he doesn't want any interference. But I also know he won't tolerate any opposition. Please, tell me. I may be able to help."

As Foster spoke about Linrock, I noticed the intense interest on Miss Barkley's face. She and Gwen both listened intently to Foster's every word, captivated by his storytelling ability. He spoke convincingly, with a certain persuasive power that betrayed his experience. And his face, once stern and hard, softened as he conveyed his noble intentions, something quite unexpected in a gun-fighting Ranger.

"Papa said you were a hunter of outlaws, a man who'd rather kill than save," she exclaimed, shocked.

Foster's face hardened once more. "My name is infamous, I'm sorry to say," he admitted.

"Have you killed men?" she asked, her eyes widening.

I could sense the tension in the air as Foster's face became a mask. He didn't answer, but I knew the truth. "Miss Barkley, I hope I won't have to," he said quietly.

His words seemed to calm her, but I knew that the situation in Linrock was far from over.

I had correctly assessed her character - young, inexperienced, but full of pride, passion, and fire. She was beautiful then, with her fair complexion. Foster was watching her, and he couldn't have missed the radiance of her beauty or the display of her quick and noble heart.

"Excuse me, Mr. Foster," she said, regaining her composure. "I apologize for my curiosity. Thank you for trusting me. Your news is distressing, but I enjoyed our conversation. You can count on me to talk to my father."

It seemed like a dismissal, so the Ranger left. I followed, without saying anything. When we reached the end of the porch and walked into the moonlight, I decided not to reveal my identity. I don't know why, but I wanted to surprise him and earn his approval. He towered over me, appearing not to notice my presence. This Ranger was a strange, distant man.

However, I remembered how earnestly he spoke to Miss Barkley, so I couldn't think of him as cold. But I must have thought he was immune to the charms of those lovely girls. Suddenly, as we walked under the shade of the cottonwood trees, he clapped his big hand on my shoulder.

"My God, Tim, she's gorgeous!" he exclaimed. Despite my shock, I hugged him. He recognized me!

"I thought you didn't swear!" I gasped. Those were my first words to Vaughn Foster, and they sounded ridiculous.

"My boy, I saw you looking for me up and down the street," he said. "I was going to help you find me tomorrow."

We shook hands, and the firm grip meant a lot. "Yes, she's beautiful, Foster," I said. "But did you see the cousin, the little girl with the bright eyes?"

Then we laughed and let go of each other's hands. "Let's go somewhere," I suggested.

"I've got a lot to tell you," I said as we made our way out into the open. The moonlight shone down on us, illuminating the white stones that dotted the landscape. We sat down in the sand, our backs against a rest, and began our conversation. I started by recounting Neal's urgent message to me, then told him about my trip to the capitol and what I had overheard in the adjutant's office. I went on to describe my interview with the officials and the spying on Colonel Barkley. I told him about Neal's directions, advice, and command, and about our ride towards San Antonio. I mentioned how I had been hired as a cowboy by Miss Barkley, and the further ride on to Sanderson, along with the incident that occurred there. Finally, I told him about how I had approached Barkley and thought it wise to involve his daughter in our plan. The conversation was long, even for me, and my voice sounded hoarse by the end.

"I told Neal I'd be lucky to get you," Foster said after a moment of silence. It was the only comment he made about my actions, the only praise I received. But the way he said it, so calmly and quietly, made me feel unworthy of such recognition. "Oh, I almost forgot," I said, relieved to be rid of the large bundle of bills I had been carrying. Foster looked surprised, but he was pleased. "The Captain loves the service," he said. "He alone understands the value of the Rangers. And the work he's devoted his life to, the good that service can do, all depends on you and me, Tim!"

I nodded, feeling gloomy. Foster paused for a moment, lost in thought. The moon was high in the sky, and a cool wind rustled the greasewood. A dog barked in the distance, and lights twinkled in the town below. I looked back up at the dark hill and thought of Gwen Langdon. Meeting Foster and coming to Linrock had not changed my feelings for her, but it seemed as if I was now lost in thought, out of reach. "Well, son, listen," Foster began.

He might even be in cahoots with the gang. But I hope not."Foster chuckled. "You're a smart one, Tim. You've got it all figured out. Now, let's get to work."I nodded, feeling the weight of the task ahead of me. Foster had given me a plan, but it was a dirty one. I had to pretend to be someone I wasn't, all while keeping up appearances with Miss Barkley. It didn't sit right with me, but I knew it was necessary for the job.As I left Foster's office, I couldn't shake the feeling that something was off about Barkley. I didn't know what it was, but I was determined to find out. This was my chance to prove myself as a Ranger, and I wasn't going to let anyone down.I spent the next few days ingratiating myself with the gang. I played cards, drank whiskey, and laughed at their jokes. It wasn't easy, but I was making progress. They were starting to trust me, and I was learning more about their operations.At night, Foster and I would meet up and discuss our findings. It was grueling work, but we were making headway. We were getting closer to the truth about Barkley and his connections to the gang.But as the days went on, I found myself growing more and more attached to Miss Barkley. She was everything Foster had said she was and more. Kind, intelligent, and beautiful. I knew I was playing a dangerous game, but I couldn't help the way I felt.As the investigation continued, I found myself torn between my duty to the Rangers and my feelings for Miss Barkley. It was a difficult balancing act, but I knew I had to stay focused. The fate of the town depended on it. And so, I continued to play my role, pretending to be someone I wasn't. But deep down, I knew that the truth would eventually come out. And when it did, I would have to face the consequences of my actions. But for now, all I could do was keep moving forward, one step at a time.

"I don't like him, but I hope we're wrong for his daughter's sake," Foster said, his eyes deep and gleaming in the moonlight as he searched my face. "You sure you're not gonna fall in love with her, son?"

"I'm positive. Why?" I asked.

"Because if you did, I'd likely have need of a new man in your place," he replied.

I pressed him for more information about Barkley, but he claimed to know no more than I did. "When a fellow has been years at this game, he has a sixth sense. Mine seldom fails me," Foster said. "I never yet faced the criminal who didn't somehow betray fear - not so much fear of me, but fear of himself, his life, his deeds. That's conscience, or if not, just realization of fate."

I wondered if that was the same fear I had seen in Barkley's face. "I'm sorry Diane Barkley came out here," I said.

Foster didn't say whether he shared that feeling or not. He was looking out at the moon-blanched level, and something in his face made me think he was thinking about the beautiful girl who might be brought to disgrace and unhappiness.

Chapter Two.

As I sat atop the corral fence, taking in the breathtaking view before me, I couldn't help but feel grateful for still being in the employ of Diane Barkley. A whole month had flown by, filled with new experiences and a sense of renewed life. It was a beautiful morning in May, the sun just beginning to peek over the horizon. The dew on the leaves and grass shimmered like diamonds in the early light, and the gentle breeze carried the sweet melody of larks. The range, a vast expanse of gray-green that grew greener as it stretched westward, undulated in rolling ridges and hollows like waves crashing into the dark, low hills that notched the blue horizon line.

Before me stood three magnificent horses, saddled and ready for the day ahead. Their sleek coats glistened in the morning light, and their muscular bodies exuded an air of strength and grace. It was a sight that would have pleased any horse lover.

As I took it all in, I couldn't help but feel a sense of contentment wash over me. Life was good, and I was grateful for the opportunity to be a part of it.

As I waited for the young ladies to arrive for their morning ride, I couldn't help but reflect on my recent experiences. In the past, I had thought I had reasons to ponder, but now I scoffed at those moments as trivial compared to what I had been through recently. It was one of those moments where I felt like an outsider looking in, skeptically observing the cowboy persona I had adopted.

My attire was the epitome of a flashy cowboy, complete with a large sombrero adorned with a silver band, a red silk scarf, a black velvet shirt popular with the Indians, an embroidered buckskin vest, corduroy pants, fringed chaps with silver buttons, and a big blue gun hanging low at my side. My boots had high heels, and my spurs boasted silver rowels. Foster, my companion, had once claimed that I was a natural actor, but I never admitted that without my infatuation for Gwen, I would never have been able to pull off this act, not even to save the Ranger service or the entire state of Texas.

The most challenging part wasn't establishing a reputation; it was dealing with the scorn of cowboys, the ridicule of gamblers, and the teasing of the young men in the town. I had earned their respect through my quick wit and ability to fight with my fists and my gun. Despite the constant influx of strangers in Linrock, I relished spending time in hotels and resorts, pretending to have a weakness for drinking, gambling, and lounging, all while making friends with the rough crowd. I was a cool, calculating machine, always observing and registering everything around me.

The hardest part of my charade was the lie I lived in the eyes of Diane Barkley and Gwen Langdon. Despite winning the sincere regard of my employer, I couldn't help feeling guilty for deceiving the two women who had captured my heart.

People around town, including her father, cousin Reuben, and other new acquaintances, had come to her with tales of my reckless behavior, urging for my dismissal. However, she refused to let me go and pleaded with me to mend my ways. Despite believing the rumors about me, she had faith in me and saw past my facade. I had fallen deeply in love with Gwen, who was indifferent towards me at times, cold at others, friendly like a comrade, and dangerously sweet. Somehow, she saw through me and knew I wasn't who I pretended to be, but she never spoke her conviction. Instead, she championed me. I wanted to confess the truth about myself to her, thinking that it was the only way to win her over. However, she had never expressed any romantic feelings towards me, despite the way she looked at me. Despite this personal turmoil, I remained loyal to Vaughn Foster and committed to our work. It had been a busy month, as we laid the foundation for our mission. My vigilance and stealthy efforts had yet to yield any evidence against Barkley, who was often absent from the home and hard to keep an eye on when he was there. Reuben Darling, who was involved in stock deals with Barkley and other men, had earned my contempt due to his heavy drinking, cruelty towards horses, and his tendency to cheat in gambling. He had also fallen in love with Diane Barkley and followed her around like a shadow when at home.

The man despised me. He treated me like dirt beneath his feet, and if he ever had to speak to me, he did so with a harshness usually reserved for dogs. Every time I caught sight of his handsome face, with its dark, half-closed eyes, I felt a hot, thick anger boiling up inside me. Foster and I spent a lot of time discussing the character and actions of Reuben Darling, who was Barkley's partner and the leader of a group of wealthy Linrock ranchers. We decided to bide our time before investigating their business practices too thoroughly. After all, this was a waiting game. From the start, it seemed that Linrock was none too pleased with Vaughn Foster's presence. But I suspected that there were some men in Linrock who secretly welcomed the Ranger's arrival. Everyone was speculating about what he was going to do, and his fame had preceded him. His mere presence had more of an impact on the wild Linrock element than an entire company of militia could have had. A thousand stories circulated about him, most of which were false. Some said he was lightning-fast on the draw and that it was certain death to face him. Others claimed he had killed thirty men, which was the wildest rumor of all. He was said to possess the gun-skill of Buck Duane, the cunning of Cheseldine, and the devilry of King Fisher, the most notorious of Texas desperadoes. His nerve and lack of fear set him apart even among a horde of bold men. At first, the vicious element with which I had begun to affiliate myself was all conjecture and no action, for fear of alerting the sharp-eyed Ranger.

During his first few days in Linrock, Foster wasn't often seen in town, but he didn't hide either. People in bars and lounges were curious about him, wondering who he was after, what he would do first, and who would draw on him first. Some even speculated about when he would be found full of lead. As time went by, those who I needed to cultivate grew more curious and impatient.

When it was leaked that Foster was trying to gather honest citizens to fight against the other element, Linrock showed its wolf teeth. People shot at Foster in the dark a few times, and he was slightly injured once. Rumors spread that Jack Blome, the local gunman, was coming to meet Foster. Linrock became divided, with some people becoming more secluded and others becoming rowdier. Strangers came and went, and a lot of money circulated. Vague rumors of rustlers, hold-ups, robberies, and murders crept in from other places, but neither Foster nor I could associate any of it with a possible gang of rustlers in Linrock. Despite this, we weren't discouraged. After three weeks, we became aware of activity around us, and we believed we would soon be on its track. My task was busy but easy, while Foster had to be careful for his life. I always reminded him of this.

As I pondered on the possibilities of the month ahead, Miss Barkley and Gwen interrupted my thoughts. My employer appeared distressed while Gwen wore her cowgirl riding costume, accentuating her curvy figure and her daring, sparkling eyes. "Good morning, Tim," Miss Barkley greeted me, scrutinizing my face. I knew I was in for a lecture, so I put on a bold, innocent front. "Did you break your promise to me?" she asked, her voice laced with disappointment. "Which one?" I retorted, more concerned about Gwen's gaze on me than Miss Barkley's reproach. "About getting drunk again," Miss Barkley replied. "I didn't break that one."

"My cousin Reuben saw you in the Hope So gambling place last night, drunk, staggering, mixing with that riffraff, on the verge of a brawl," she continued. "Miss Barkley, with all due respect to Mr.

Darling, I want to say that he has a strange wish to lower me in the eyes of you ladies," I protested, trying to sound spirited. "Tim, were you drunk?" she demanded. "No. I should think you needn't ask me that. Didn't you ever see a man the morning after a carouse?"

Apparently, she had seen such a sight before, and I stood before them, fresh, clean-shaven, and clear-eyed. Even Gwen's saucy face grew pensive. The only thing she ever asked of me was not to drink, as the Barkley family had a hard time with the habit. "Tim, you look just as nice as I'd want you to," Miss Barkley said, her tone uncertain. "I don't know what to think. They tell me things. You deny. Whom shall I believe? Reuben swore he saw you."

"Miss Barkley, did I ever lie to you?" I asked. "Not to my knowledge," she replied. I looked at her, and she understood what I meant. "Reuben has lied to me. That day at Sanderson. And since, too, I fear."

"Miss Barkley, are you calling him a liar?" I asked, trying to diffuse the tension. Gwen moved closer, holding the bridle rein of her horse. "Tim, cousin Reuben isn't the only one who saw you. Burt Waters told me the same thing," Gwen said nervously. It seemed like she wanted to believe me, but wasn't sure. "Waters! So he talks behind my back. I won't say anything about him, but do you really believe I was drunk?" I asked, feeling frustrated.

"I'm afraid I do, Tim," Miss Barkley replied reluctantly. Was she testing me? "Look, Miss Barkley," I burst out, "why don't you just let me go? I'm not claiming to be a saint, but you don't believe me at all. I'm pretty bad, I'll admit that. I've done my fair share of gambling and fighting, but I did keep my promise to you. Now, discharge me so I can call on Mr. Burt Waters."

Miss Barkley looked alarmed, and Gwen turned pale. They both seemed to think I was a dangerous cowboy who was only being held back by their kindness. "No, please don't go," Gwen pleaded. "Diane, don't let him go!"

"Tim, please don't get angry," Miss Barkley said, putting a soft hand on my arm. It thrilled me, but also made me feel like a villain. "I won't discharge you. I need you, and so does Gwen. After all, what you do outside of here is none of my business. Didn't you ever have a sister, Tim?"

I stayed silent, not wanting to lie again. But the situation was too good to pass up. "Miss Barkley," I started hesitantly, "I've made mistakes in the past. But I've been trying my best to be good here and make you happy."

Recently, I've been going down a bad path. Not drunk, but heading that way. Who knows what I'll do soon if my problem isn't fixed.

"Tim! What's wrong?" asked my friend Gwen.

"You know what's going on with me," I replied hastily. "Anyone could see it."

Gwen blushed furiously. Miss Barkley looked at me with understanding. "I've fallen in love with Miss Gwen. I'm crazy about her. It's killing me to see these guys flirting with her," I confessed.

"If you're crazy about me, you don't have to say it!" Gwen exclaimed, her face turning red and white. "I want to stop your flirting one way or another. I've been serious. I wasn't flirting. I begged you to-"

"You never did," interrupted Gwen furiously. That hint had been a spark.

"I couldn't have dreamed it," I protested, wanting to be serious but also feeling amused. "That day when I didn't ask-"

"If I remember correctly, you didn't ask anything," she replied, anger and sarcasm mixing with amusement. "But, Gwen, I meant to. You understood me? Say you didn't believe I could take that liberty without honorable intentions."

Gwen couldn't handle it and quickly mounted her horse, taking off like a bolt. "Stop me if you can," she called back with a mischievous grin. "Tim, go after her," said Miss Barkley. "In that mood, she'll ride to Sanderson. My dear fellow, don't stare so. I understand many things now. Gwen is a flirt. She would drive any man mad. Tim, I've grown to like you a lot in a short time. If you give up drinking and gambling, maybe you'll have a chance with her. Hurry now, go after her."

I quickly mounted my horse and spurred it to catch up with Gwen's.

She rode out in the open, giving her horse free rein. Even if I had wanted to catch up with her, it would have been nearly impossible within the first five miles. Gwen had one of the fastest horses on the range and she rode like a pro. Every now and then, she looked back over her shoulder, noticing that I was gaining on her. Gwen was a lover of horses, races, and winning. I had the good fortune of riding with her alone more than once. Miss Barkley enjoyed riding as well, but she was not as daring as Gwen. Whenever she joined us, there was never a race. Whenever Gwen and I were out on our own, she always made me ride to keep up with her or else I would lose her in the horizon. This morning, I wanted her to experience complete freedom and to feel that I could not catch her even if I tried. Maybe my declaration to Miss Barkley had unleashed my strongest emotions. Whatever the reason, this ride was like no other, with the sky so blue, the scenery so vast and enchanting, and the wind so sweet. It felt as though the breeze was carrying the fragrance of Gwen Langdon's hair. I rode on like I had never ridden before. Horses grazed and whinnied as I passed by, jack-rabbits hopped and hid in the tall grass, and a wolf slinked away from a herd of cattle nearby. Far in the distance, the low, dark lines of mountains rose to the west, always seeming to hold a mysterious secret that I needed to uncover.

The ride was strange because I couldn't shake the haunting feeling that my business on the frontier was deadly. It was in such contrast to the dreamy and futile longings that consumed my thoughts. At any moment, I could be revealed as a Ranger and my disguise would be stripped away. Gwen led the way across the wide plain and up to the top of a ridge, where she waited for me, tired but victorious. I took my time reaching the summit, wondering how Gwen would receive me after my embarrassing display in front of her cousin. I had no reason to be hopeful, but to my surprise, she greeted me in her sweetest mood, with a hint of shyness I had never seen before.

"Tim, I gave you a run for your money that time," she said. "Ten miles and you never caught me!"

"But you had a head start. I've had my fair share of trouble trying to beat you on an even playing field," I replied, knowing that Gwen was susceptible to flattery when it came to her riding skills.

"In a longer race, I was afraid you'd beat me. Tim, I've learned to ride out here. Back home, I never had the space to ride a horse. Just look at this. Miles and miles of level, green land. Little hills with black bunches of trees. Not a soul in sight. Even the town is hidden in the green. It's all wild and lonely. Isn't it glorious, Tim?"

"Lately, it's been getting to me," I replied solemnly. Gwen and I gazed out over the sea of gray-green, taking in the undulating waves of the ground in the distance. These rides had taught me to appreciate the beauty of the lonely plains, but when I looked at Gwen, I couldn't help but focus on her. The scenery could wait.

As I gazed upon her, I attempted to discern that unique quality that set her apart from others, but it evaded me. With a rose in her cheeks, hair blowing in the wind, and her eyes now serious instead of teasing, she only appeared more beautiful than usual. I dismounted from my horse, ostensibly to tighten the saddle girths on hers, but I took my time with the task. When she looked down at me, I sensed a subtle shift in her demeanor, a softness and dangerous sweetness that rarely manifested, mingled with a deeper sense of character and womanhood that I had never before perceived in her.

"Tim, it wasn't nice to tell Diane that," she spoke, breaking the silence.

"Nice! It was, oh, I'd like to swear!" I exclaimed, realizing the source of my miserable feelings. "But now I understand. I was jealous, Gwen. I'm sorry. I apologize."

Gwen removed her gloves, and her hand, small and shapely, rested on her knee, near me. I took it in mine, and she allowed it, though she averted her gaze, the color in her cheeks deepening. "I can forgive that," she murmured. "But the lie. Jealousy doesn't excuse a lie."

"You mean what I suggested to your cousin?" I clarified, attempting to meet her gaze. "That was the devil in me. But it's true."

"How can it be true when you never said a word about it?" she challenged. "Diane believed what you said. I know she thinks me horrid."

"No, she doesn't. And as for what I said, or meant to say, which is essentially the same thing, how did you interpret my actions? I hope not in the same way as you interpret Darling's or the other fellow's."

Gwen fell silent, her complexion now a little pallid, and I discerned that I didn't need to mention the other fellows any further. The change in her was palpable, and it spurred me to give in to the fervent and ardent side of myself entirely. "Gwen, I love you."

My actions may have confused you, but let me clarify. I was consumed by both love and jealousy. Will you marry me?" Gwen remained silent, but her stubborn nature was nowhere to be seen. I slowly pulled her towards me, a gesture she could have easily resisted, yet she slipped from her horse and into my arms. In that moment, I felt the sweet certainty of her kissing me of her own volition. She was bashful yet yielding, allowing herself to be held but not completely undone. Perhaps I was too rough, for she cried out and pleaded for me to release her. I obliged, but not entirely.

"Gwen, you still haven't given me an answer," I pleaded tenderly. "Do you love me?"

"I think so," she whispered.

"Gwen, will you marry me?"

She disengaged herself from me and sat up straight, her chest heaving. "No, Tim," she finally said, regaining her composure. "But if I love you, why won't I marry you?" I interrupted, but her expression silenced me. "I can't just promise to marry you. I don't even know your last name. You're not a reliable man. You drink, gamble, and fight. You'll end up killing someone, and then I won't love you anymore. Besides, there's something about you that I can't trust."

I could feel my face darken, and my hope and happiness quickly dissipated. But before I could say anything, Gwen placed a kind hand on my shoulder. "I'm sorry if I hurt you. But I had to tell you why I couldn't be engaged to you. I know your intentions are genuine, but I just can't trust you. You're not good enough for me."

"I had no right to ask you to marry me," I said humbly. "Gwen, please don't think I'm too proud," she hesitated. "I wouldn't care who you were if only I could respect you. Some things about you are amazing, you're such a man, that's why I care. But you gamble. You drink and I hate that. They say you're dangerous, and I am constantly afraid you'll hurt someone. Remember, Tim, I'm not from Texas." This regret from Gwen, this faltering distress in causing me pain, was such a sweet assurance that she loved me, more than she knew, that I was divided between extremes of emotion. "Will you wait? Will you give me a chance? After all, maybe I'm not as bad as I seem." "Oh, if only you weren't! Tim, are you asking me to trust you?" "I beg you, dearest. Trust me and wait." "Wait? What for? Are you really honest, Tim? Or are you what Reuben calls you, a drunken cowboy, a gambler, sharp with the cards, a gunfighter?" My face grew cold as I felt the blood drain from it. At that moment, the mention of Reuben Darling fixed my hatred for him once and for all. It was bitter indeed that I could not give him a lie. But what could I do? The character Darling gave me was scarcely worse than what I had chosen to represent. I had to acknowledge the justice of his claim, but I still hated him. "Gwen, I ask you to trust me despite my reputation." "You're asking me a lot," she replied. "Yes, it's too much. Let it be then only this, you'll wait. And while you wait, promise not to flirt with Darling and Waters." "Tim, I won't let Reuben or any of them so much as dare touch me," she declared in girlish earnestness, her voice rising.

"I'll make a deal with you," Gwen said, her voice soft and pleading. "If you promise not to go into those saloons anymore, I promise to do the same." Her words tugged at my heartstrings. I couldn't resist the way her face lit up with hope, her eyes glistening with tears.

But I couldn't give in. My mission in Linrock was too important. I couldn't let Gwen's charm distract me from the dark nature of my work. I wanted to tell her everything, to spill the truth, but it wasn't my secret to share. So, I kept my promise and stayed silent.

Gwen's expression shifted from hopeful to disappointed. I could see the hurt in her eyes, and it made my heart ache. But then she turned her scorn on me, and I couldn't help feeling angry.

"That's too much to promise all at once," I protested lamely, knowing my words were weak.

"Tim, a promise like that is nothing if a man loves a girl," Gwen retorted. "Don't make any more love to me, please, unless you want me to laugh at you. And don't feel such terrible trouble if you happen to see me flirting occasionally."

Her mocking laughter stung, and I felt a surge of bitterness rise in my throat. "All right. I'll take my medicine," I replied bitterly. "I'll certainly never make love to you again. And I'll stand it if I happen to see Waters kiss you, or any other decent fellow. But look out how you let that damned backbiter Darling fool around you!"

My words came out in a quick, fierce torrent, my eyes locked onto hers. Gwen paled at my intensity, and for a moment, I regretted my outburst. But then I remembered the dark purpose of my mission, and my resolve hardened. I couldn't let myself be swayed by Gwen's charm, no matter how much it tore at my heart.

My subtle insinuation failed to quell her fury. She flipped her head and galloped away. I trailed a short distance behind her as we made our way back to the ranch, a ten-mile journey. Once we arrived at the corrals, she dismounted and handed her horse over to Dick. Without so much as a nod or goodbye, she headed towards the house. I, too, was in no mood for pleasantries and decided to head into town. However, upon turning onto the main street, I was immediately distracted by a commotion outside the town hall. The noise and excitement seemed to be connected to Barkley, the mayor of Linrock, who held court in the hall once a month. I had to push my way through the crowd to get inside. Once I was in, I saw that most of the crowd was outside, not interested in entering. Foster, Barkley, and Darling were all present, along with a dozen or so other men, all shouting excitedly. I moved closer to the front but didn't bother trying to hear what was being said. Barkley sat at a table on a platform, alongside Hanford Owens, the county judge, and Gorsech, one of his sheriffs. There were also several other familiar faces and a few strangers, all dusty horsemen.

Foster stood apart from the group, his hair messy and his shirt unbuttoned. He looked calm and tough. When our eyes met, I knew that the moment we had been waiting for had finally arrived. Barkley banged on the table to get everyone's attention. Despite being the mayor, he struggled to settle the commotion. Eventually, things quieted down and I overheard that Foster had interrupted a meeting in the hall.

"Foster, what are you doing here?" Barkley demanded. "Isn't this a court? Aren't you the mayor of Linrock?" Foster replied in a loud and clear voice, making it evident that he wanted everyone outside to hear.

"Yes," Barkley answered, appearing as hard as flint. However, I could sense his keen interest in what Foster had to say. I knew then that Foster's intention was to make Barkley stand out before the crowd as either the real mayor of Linrock or as a man whose office was a sham.

"I've arrested a criminal," Foster announced. "Bud Rassmussen. I charge him with assaulting Jim Dempsey and attempting robbery, if not murder. Rassmussen had a questionable past here, which the court will know if it keeps a record."

I then noticed Rassmussen cowering on a bench, looking visibly shaken. He had been a regular at the gambling dens, the type of person I never trusted. Jim Dempsey, the restaurant owner, was also present and upon closer inspection, I saw that he was pale and had blood on his face. I knew Jim; I liked him and had tried to befriend him. The last sentence of Foster's speech stung, and I knew I had correctly judged his motive. I began to get excited about the situation.

"What's the word on the street, Bud? Speak up for yourself," barked Barkley. Rassmussen stood up, glancing nervously at Foster, and shuffled forward a few steps towards the mayor. He had a sinister appearance but lacked the courage of a rustler. "It's not true, Barkley," he began in a loud voice. "I went to Dempsey's for food. Some stranger I've never seen before came in from the hall and attacked him, wrestling him to the ground. Then this big

Ranger came and arrested me. I didn't do anything. This Ranger just wants to arrest someone. That's what I reckon, Barkley."

"What do you have to say about this, Dempsey?" Barkley asked sharply. "I remind you that you once lied in court and were punished for it."

Why did I sense a hint of threat or danger in Barkley's reminder? Dempsey got up from the bench and used his unsteady hand to support himself. He was no longer young and seemed to be broken in health and spirit. He had a head injury. "I don't have much to say," he replied. "The Ranger brought me here. I told him I didn't take my problems to court. Besides, I can't swear it was Rassmussen who hit me."

Barkley whispered something to Judge Owens, and the judge nodded his bushy head. "Bud, you're free to go," Barkley said bluntly. "The rest of you, get out of here."

He completely ignored the Ranger. This was his way of rejecting Foster's advances and rebuffing the interfering Ranger Service. If Barkley was corrupt, he had a lot of nerve. I almost thought he was above suspicion. However, his nonchalant attitude, his air of finality, his authoritative assurance, and the slight tension around his mouth and the slow paling of his olive skin were all telltale signs to my experienced eyes.

He had crossed paths with Vaughn Foster, a famous Texas Ranger, and had blocked his way. The man seemed to understand the gravity of what he had done. I studied Barkley and noticed his intense curiosity. Suddenly, Bud Rassmussen coughed and took a couple of steps towards the door. Foster called out, "Hold on!" It was like a bugle-call, stopping Rassmussen in his tracks. Foster accused Rassmussen of attacking Dempsey, and Barkley was forced to confront the Ranger Service's idea of law. He didn't hesitate and declared that they wouldn't aid or abet or accept any Ranger Service west of the Pecos. Foster called him out on his lie and produced letters from Linrock citizens begging for Ranger Service. Barkley was at a loss for words. Foster demanded Barkley's help, and when he refused, he declared that he would work alone and take Rassmussen to Del Rio in irons. Reuben Darling, who had no apparent reason to be angry, rushed up to the table and cursed Barkley. Barkley shoved him back and demanded to see Foster's warrant. Foster replied that he didn't need one to make an arrest and that Barkley was ignorant of the power of Texas Rangers. Barkley bellowed that they couldn't take Rassmussen without papers.

Foster responded to Barkley's threat with a confident, "He won't. You won't be able to pull any of your Ranger tricks out here. I'll make sure of it." Barkley's passionate response seemed to be what Foster was waiting for. He wanted to force Barkley's hand and make his stance clear to the town. Foster stepped back from the crowd and in a swift motion, his guns were drawn. It was like watching a transformation - Foster, the Ranger, was ready for a showdown. I was thrilled to see him in action. I couldn't wait to join in!

"Folks! Listen up!" Foster shouted. "I need your help to arrest this criminal who is being protected by Barkley, the mayor of Linrock.

This will be reported to the Adjutant General in Austin. Barkley, don't try anything stupid."

Barkley sat there, fuming with anger. Foster then called out to Rassmussen, ordering him to come forward. Rassmussen, looking nervous, obeyed. Foster took out a pair of handcuffs from his pocket and handed them to Gorsech. "Put these on Rassmussen," he commanded. Rassmussen was then escorted to stand next to Foster.

I was amazed at how quickly Foster's commands were followed. He must have sensed that there was danger in the air, and he wanted to make sure everyone knew he meant business. It was a tense moment, and I could feel the weight of the situation. Foster was a man of action, and his courage was contagious. I forgot that I was a part of this and not just a spectator.

"Foster, you've shown your cards," spoke Barkley, his voice low and carrying throughout the room. "Any honest citizen of Linrock can see that your hand is a damn poor one! You're going to hear me speak plainly. Your accusations against my office are baseless. In the two years that I've been mayor, we have made progress in combating rustlers. Linrock is no longer a safe haven for them. As for sending prisoners to Del Rio or Austin, we have a small jail that is not equipped for long-term holding. We have had to rely on neighboring towns for that.

"There have been unfortunate incidents in our town, but we have done our best to bring the perpetrators to justice. As for the law-suits in my court, I assure you that they were handled fairly and impartially. I do not play favorites.

"I will not stand for these baseless accusations any longer. If you have evidence of any wrongdoing on my part, then present it. Otherwise, I suggest you leave this hall and let us get back to the business of running this town."

Barkley paused, his eyes scanning the room. The tension was palpable, and I could sense the anger simmering just below the surface. But no one made a move.

"Foster, you have had your say," continued Barkley. "Now it's time for me to speak. I have worked tirelessly to make Linrock a safer and more prosperous place. I will not let your words tarnish my reputation. If you have any real concerns, then bring them to me in private. But do not come into my hall and make baseless accusations."

Barkley's words hung in the air, and I could sense that the crowd was starting to turn against Foster. He had overplayed his hand, and now he was paying the price. The meeting ended without any further incident, and as I made my way out of the hall, I couldn't help but feel a sense of relief. The tension had been thick, but Barkley had handled it with aplomb. He was a true leader, and I knew that Linrock was in good hands.

Chapter Three.

As Foster exited the hall, shoving Rassmussen ahead of him and creating a path through the throng of people, it became impossible to keep an eye on everyone. However, he appeared to disregard the individuals trailing behind him at this point.

Any friend of Rassmussen's among the dangerous crowd could have pulled out a gun. I wondered if Foster was aware of my watchful eye on those men behind him. If any of them made a sudden move, it would have been fatal. However, I realized that Foster trusted the effect his bravery had on people. It was his ability to intimidate regular men that explained his many accomplishments. Yet, it was his courage to confront desperate men that made him exceptional. The group followed Foster and his prisoner down the main street, observing him secure a team and a buckboard before driving off towards Sanderson. Only then did the crowd seem to fully comprehend what had transpired.

Finally, my opportunity presented itself. From the silence of some men, I sensed something important. From the hurried departure of others, I gathered that something significant had taken place. From the hushed, whispering lips of others, I heard words that I needed to hear. To my surprise, the smaller part of the crowd was the violent, threatening, and complaining group. Thus, I separated Linrock into two parts: the lawless and the ones who wanted law. However, for some reason, the latter group did not dare to speak up. How could Foster and I convince them to join our cause openly? If we could do so, Linrock would be free of violence before the year was up, and Captain Neal's Ranger Service would be saved for the state. I went from place to place, corner to corner, and bar to bar, watching, listening, and recording. It wasn't until long after sunset that I returned to the ranch. The excitement had preceded me, and everyone was speculating. I hurried through my supper to escape the questioning and continue my espionage. Finally, I went out to the front of the house.

The warm evening air wafted through the open doors of Barkley's large sitting room, casting a soft twilight glow over the space. The only illumination came from a few lamps scattered about, their light flickering in the shadows. Barkley and Darling were nowhere to be found, having not returned for supper. I longed to eavesdrop on their conversation, and made plans to do so once they returned. When the sound of a buckboard drew near and they stepped out, I hid myself in the bushes, catching only a fleeting glimpse of Barkley as he entered the house. He seemed calm and collected, dignified even in the face of insult. I missed my chance to observe Darling, as they entered the house without a word and shut the door behind them.

I stationed myself on the porch, hidden in the shadows near a window, hoping to hear what Barkley and Darling might say about Foster if they visited the girls that evening. I needed to know whether Diane Barkley had been told the truth about him. I waited patiently in the darkness, accustomed to this sort of stakeout, until I saw the small lamp inside flicker to life, signaling someone's approach. I heard Miss Barkley's anxious voice, "Something's happened, surely, Gwen. Papa just met me in the hall and didn't speak. He seemed pale, worried."

Gwen replied, "Cousin Reuben looked like a thundercloud. For once, he didn't try to kiss me. Something's happened. Well, Diane, this has been a bad day for me, too."

I couldn't help but feel a twinge of sympathy for Gwen. Her sigh was so full of pathos that it brought me out of my own unpleasant task of spying and speculating. Diane responded in an amused tone, "Bad for you, too?"

"Oh, I forgot to mention earlier. You and Tim had a fight," said Diane.

"A fight? We fought like crazy. I never want to speak to him again," replied Gwen.

"So your little fling with Tim is over?" asked Diane.

"Yes," sighed Gwen. "It started fast and ended quickly. We don't really know much about Tim."

"Diane, I have to admit, despite everything, I respect him now. I cared about him a lot," added Gwen.

"My dear, your love interests are like summer flowers. I thought your flirting with Tim might lead somewhere, but he seems so different now from when we first met him. Occasionally, I get the impression I had of him after he saved me from violence. He's strange. Maybe it's because of his infatuation with you. He's in love with you, and I'm afraid of what may come of it," said Diane.

"Diane, mark my words, he'll do something terrible to Reuben," whispered Gwen. "He promised he would if Reuben tried to get with me again."

"Oh dear, Gwen, what can we do? These men are wild. Reuben makes my life miserable, and he teases you," replied Diane.

"I don't call it teasing. Reuben wants to be intimate with me. He'd chase after any woman," declared Gwen.

"That's not a very flattering compliment to me, Cousin Gwen," laughed Diane.

"I disagree," said Gwen stubbornly. "It's true. He's infatuated. And when he's drunk and tries to kiss me, I can't stand him."

"Gwen, it seems like you want Tim to do something terrible to Reuben," said Diane, half-jokingly.

"Part of me does, and part of me doesn't," replied Gwen. "But I'm scared of Tim. I have a feeling something's going to happen between him and Reuben."

Suddenly, they heard quick footsteps in the hallway. Diane thought she recognized them.

"Hey, girls!" Darling's voice sounded different, lacking its usual cheerfulness. There was a pause, and I could imagine the expression on Darling's face turning sour. "Reuben, what's wrong?" Diane asked after a while. "I've never seen Dad like this before, nor have I seen you so worried. Tell me, what happened?" "Well, Diane, we had a problem today," replied Darling, letting out a blunt and expressive laugh. "Problem?" Both girls echoed curiously. "Problem? We had to face a terrible injustice," added Darling, his voice becoming more passionate. "Listen, girls. I'll tell you everything." He coughed, clearing his throat in a way that indicated he had been drinking. I hid deeper in the shadows, preparing to listen intently. One slip of the tongue from Darling could give Foster the lead he needed. "It happened at the town hall," Darling began quickly. "Your father, Judge Owens, and I were there, having a meeting with three ranchers from out of town. Suddenly, we heard gunshots from somewhere, but they weren't close by. Then we heard loud voices outside. A crowd had gathered outside the hall, and men were running in, shouting. We thought there was a fire. Then Ranger Foster walked in, dragging a guy named Rassmussen. We couldn't hear what was being said because of the noise. Finally, your father restored order. Foster had arrested Rassmussen for allegedly assaulting a restaurant owner named Dempsey. But Dempsey didn't accuse anyone and didn't know who had attacked him. Rassmussen was clearly innocent and was released. But then this gun-toting Ranger pulled his guns on the court and stopped the proceedings." When Darling paused, I heard him take a deep breath. He was far from calm.

Foster had the entire hall in a state of panic as he hurled insults at everyone. He claimed that law was a joke in Linrock and that the court was a sham. He insisted that there was no law to be found in the town. Foster even went as far as to say that Diane's father, who was the mayor, should be impeached. According to him, the mayor only made arrests for minor offenses and was too afraid to deal with the rustlers, highwaymen, and murderers. Foster believed that the mayor either didn't care or was too scared to act. The ranger also accused the mayor of using his position to cheat ranchers and cattlemen out of their money in lawsuits.

Diane was deeply disturbed and angry at Foster's words. She couldn't believe that someone would insult her father in such a way. Darling, who was also present, explained that Foster was a ranger and that the ranger service wanted to rule western Texas. He claimed that many rangers were just as bad as the outlaws they hunted, and some were even former outlaws themselves. Foster was one of the worst rangers, according to Darling. He was smart and cunning, which made him even more dangerous. Darling was convinced that Foster wanted to kill the mayor and would have done so if the mayor had made any sudden moves.

Diane was outraged by Foster's behavior and called him a ruffian. Darling tried to console her by saying that Foster had failed in Linrock and was desperate for attention. He also pointed out that Foster was known for seeking notoriety and making inflammatory statements. Darling was worried that Foster's words would turn the people of Linrock against the mayor and make enemies for them.

Diane was not afraid of Foster's insinuations and stood up for her father. She didn't care what Foster said and was confident that her father had done nothing wrong. She was determined to protect her family's reputation and wouldn't let Foster's words get to her.

After a moment of consideration, it was clear that no one would be influenced by Foster's accusations. "Don't worry, Reuben," said the concerned Darling. "Tell Papa not to worry. After all these years, he can't be hurt by the words of an adventurer."

Reuben disagreed. "Yes, he can be hurt. The frontier is a strange place. There are many bitter men here, men who have failed at ranching. And your father has been exceptionally successful. Foster has spread some poison, and it will spread."

There was a brief silence, during which Darling paced the floor, visibly worried. "Cousin Reuben," Gwen suddenly asked, "what happened to Foster and his prisoner?" Gwen's inquisitive nature and changing points of view made it typical of her to ask a question that would be unpleasant for Darling to answer.

I was amused and thrilled at the same time. Gwen may have been a flirt, but she was no fool. "What happened to them? Ha! Foster bluffed the whole town, at least all of those who had heard the mayor's order to discharge Rassmussen," growled Darling. "He took Rassmussen and rode off to Del Rio to jail him."

"Reuben!" exclaimed Diane. "So this Ranger was able to arrest Rassmussen, the man who Father discharged, and take him to jail?"

"Exactly. That's the toughest part..." Darling trailed off abruptly, then broke out fiercely. "But, by God, he'll never come back!"

Darling's slow pacing quickened, and he left the parlor, leaving behind a silence that spoke volumes about the impact of his ominous prediction. "Gwen, what did he mean?" asked Diane in a hushed tone.

"Foster will be killed," replied Gwen, just as quietly. "Killed! That magnificent man! Ah, I forgot. Gwen, my thoughts are jumbled. I should be happy if someone kills my father's defamer. But, oh, I can't be!"

This bloody frontier is making me sick. Papa doesn't want me to stay for good. And no wonder. Should I go back? I hate to show cowardice.

"You know, Gwen, that Texas Ranger really caught my eye. I have to admit, I was impressed by him. He had this incredible presence about him. But it's crazy to think that such a great man could be so corrupt at heart. It's hard to believe how little we truly know about people. I had this whole dream about Vaughn Foster, and now I'm ashamed of myself for even thinking about it."

The next morning, I woke up feeling like my old self again. I was active and engaged, and I had a feeling that big things were on the horizon. Gwen was still on my mind, but more as a source of sadness than anything else. Maybe my failure as a lover would lead to success as an officer. I put my thoughts about Barkley and Darling on hold until Foster returned. I wasn't worried about Darling's comment that Foster might not come back. I'd heard plenty of rumors like that about Rangers before. But I didn't see anyone in Linrock who could take down Foster. Since Miss Barkley and

Gwen weren't interested in riding, I had even more freedom to explore. I headed down to town and walked into Jim Dempsey's place, whistling cheerily. Jim always welcomed me, both for my company and for the money I spent. I bought a handful of cigars and gave some to Jim. "How's it going, Jim?" I asked. "I'm feeling as well as can be expected," he replied. Jim had a bandage around his head, but it didn't cover the lump where he'd been hit. He looked a little pale, but he was still sharp. "That was a terrible hit Rassmussen gave you," I said, still cheerful.

"Listen, Jim, I ain't accusing Rassmussen," I said, looking at him thoughtfully. "I know you're a good sport and wouldn't send someone up for nothing. But let me tell you, Rassmussen got what he deserved. I saw the look on his face when he spoke at Barkley's court. He lied, plain and simple. And if it was me instead of that Ranger, I would have settled it with Rassmussen myself."

Jim seemed agitated by my strong statement of friendship. "Hey, Tim, that's between us, okay?" I continued. "I'm not a fool, and even though I talk a lot when I'm drunk, I know when to keep my mouth shut. In some parts of Texas, it's smart to stay quiet. And between you and me, as friends, I'm leaning towards Foster's side of the fence."

I lit a cigar and noticed Dempsey give a quick start, as if he had just had a sudden realization. I turned to him and met his gaze. I had a feeling I had uncovered something important. "It's funny, Tim, seeing as you're siding with the gang Foster's bound to fight," Dempsey remarked.

"Yeah, well, I'm a gambler at heart," I replied. "If I can't gamble with gentlemen, I'll gamble with rustlers."

Dempsey gave another slight start and hid his eyes. "Well, Tim, I've heard you're pretty slick," he said with a dry laugh.

"You catch on quick, Jim," I said, a sly smile spreading on my face. "I'm good on the draw, with cards and guns. And soon enough, I'll have a chance to prove it."

Dempsey chuckled. "I reckon that talk's just hot air," he said.

But I knew better. I had a feeling that soon enough, Dempsey would see just how good I was on the draw.

"You're leaning towards the Ranger's side of the fence," said one man to another.

"But, Jim, wasn't he game? What did you think of that stand? He bluffed the whole gang! The way he called Barkley, why, it was great! The justice of that call doesn't bother me. It was Foster's nerve that got me. That would warm any man's blood," replied the other man.

There was a little red in Dempsey's pale cheeks and the first man saw him swallow hard. "Say, don't you work for Barkley?" he asked.

"Me? I guess not. I'm Miss Barkley's man. He and Darling have tried to fire me many times."

"That so?" Dempsey said curiously. "What for?"

"Too many silver trimmings on me, Jim. And I pack my gun low down."

"Well, those two don't go together out here," replied Dempsey. "But I haven't seen anyone shoot off the trimmings."

"Maybe it'll commence, Jim, as soon as I stop buying drinks. Talking about work, who would you say Rassmussen works for?"

"I didn't say," replied Dempsey.

"Well, say so now, can't you? Jim, you're powerful peevish today. It's the bump on your head. Who does Rassmussen work for?"

"When he works at all, which sure isn't often, he rides for Barkley."

"Humph! Seems to me, Jim, that Barkley's the whole circus round Linrock. I was sore the other day to find I was losing good money at Barkley's faro game. Sure, if I'd won I wouldn't have been sorry, eh? But I was surprised to hear some scully say Barkley owned the Hope So dive."

"I've heard he owned considerable property hereabouts," replied Jim constrainedly.

"Humph again! Why, Jim, you know it, only like every other scully you meet in this town, you're afraid to open your mouth about Barkley. Get me straight, Jim Dempsey. I don't care a damn for Colonel Mayor Barkley."

"I wouldn't hesitate to pull a gun on him just as fast as I would on any rustler in Pecos," I said with a hint of bravado.

"Talk is cheap, kid," Dempsey replied dismissively, but his face flushed with anger.

"I know, I know," I said, trying to calm myself down. "Sometimes my temper gets the best of me. But Jim, not everyone knows that Barkley owns the Hope So, right?"

"Oh, it's well-known in Pecos," Dempsey said. "But Barkley's name isn't directly connected to the place. Blandy runs it."

"I can't stand Blandy," I said. "His faro game is rigged, or I'm a crazy horse. I know there are plenty of crooked dealers out there, but Blandy is a snake. He never looks you in the eye and always has a sneaky way about him. The Hope So should be run by a stand-up guy like you, Jim."

"Thanks, Tim," Dempsey replied, his voice a little hoarse. "Did you know that I used to run the place?"

"No way!" I exclaimed. "You did?"

"Yep," Dempsey said. "I built the place, added onto it twice, and owned it for eleven years."

"Well, I'll be damned," I said, genuinely surprised. "Why aren't you running it now, then?"

"I lost it," Dempsey said, his voice heavy with emotion. "It was two years ago, in March. Barkley and I were in a big cattle deal together. We got the stock, but my share of eighteen hundred head was rustled. I owed Barkley, and he pushed me. It ended up in a lawsuit, and I lost everything."

Looking at Dempsey, I could see the pain and defeat in his eyes. Despite his failure to meet his obligation, he had been swindled, and it was clear that it still hurt him deeply.

All that he had been suppressing, all the passion that would have been evident if his spirit hadn't been broken, was exposed for me to see. Now I understood the reason for his bitterness. However, I didn't want to inquire about his reluctance and fear, or openly accuse Barkley just yet. I figured I would consult with Foster and learn more at a later time.

"Jim, that was some hard luck. It sure was tough," I sympathized. "But you're taking it like a champ. The wheel turns!"

"Now, Jim, the real reason I came to see you is because I need some advice. I have a little money saved up, and I want to invest it. I was thinking of buying some stock or maybe even investing in a rancher's herd. But I need your help finding an honest and trustworthy rancher. I don't want to make any deals with rustlers who ride in the dark. I have a hunch that Linrock is full of them."

"Well, Tim, I'm lucky enough to know a couple of ranchers who are above suspicion," Jim replied emotionally. "Frank Morton and Si Zimmer have been my friends and neighbors for as long as I can remember. And they're still my friends. You can trust them. But if you want my advice, I wouldn't invest in any stock right now."

"Why not?"

"Because any newcomer who buys stock in Pecos these days will get rustled quicker than they can say Jack Robinson. The new cattlemen and pioneers are easy targets, but they have to learn the ropes. They don't know anyone or anything. And the old ranchers are wise and angry. They would fight if they..."

"What?" I interrupted.

"If they knew who was rustling the stock?"

"No?"

"If they had the nerve?"

"Not necessarily."

"What then?"

As I left Dempsey's, the word "leader" echoed through my mind. I imagined a group of rugged, determined cattlemen riding fearlessly behind Vaughn Foster. Lost in thought, I strolled past my old haunts until a booming voice interrupted my musings. It was Morton, the rancher Jim had mentioned to me before. He was a jolly man with a robust frame and a ruddy face.

After exchanging greetings, I suggested we grab a drink. Morton declined, citing his responsibilities on the ranch. I jokingly asked if he would sell me his land, but he laughed and said he wished he could. As his horses grew restless, I confided in him that I had some money to invest in stock. He seemed skeptical of me at first, but I assured him that I was sober and sincere.

I challenged Morton's assumptions about me, insisting that he had misjudged my intelligence and potential. Although he seemed interested in my proposal, he remained cautious. I persisted, eager to prove myself and make a deal. The cards had been running lucky for me, and I didn't want to squander my chance at success.

"Can you set me up as a stockman with my own little herd?" I asked, hoping to start my own business.

Morton looked at me skeptically. "It's strange to hear this coming from Barkley's cowboy," he remarked. "I'm not part of his outfit. My job is with Miss Barkley. She's great, but her father? No way. He's been after me for weeks. I won't last long. That's why I want to start up for myself."

"Dempsey sent you to me, didn't he?" Morton asked, referring to Jim Dempsey. "Poor old Jim. Well, Tim, to be honest with you, it would be foolish to buy cattle now. I don't want to take your money and see you lose out. You'd be better off going back across the Pecos where the rustlers aren't as strong. I haven't had more than 2,500 head of stock for ten years. The rustlers let me keep a breeding herd. Kind of them, isn't it?"

"It's kind of them, but all I hear about is rustlers," I replied impatiently. "I haven't lived long in a rustler-run county. Who's leading the gang anyway?"

Morton looked at me with an amused smile. "I hear a lot about Jack Blome and Snecker. Everyone calls them out-and-out bad. Do they lead this mysterious gang?"

"I think Blome and Snecker like to think of themselves as boss rustlers, like gun throwers," Morton said. "But that's just for show.

The real brains behind the rustler gang hereabouts are much smarter than that."

"Maybe Blome and Snecker are just distractions," I suggested. "Perhaps there's more to this rustler gang than just their fame."

Morton snapped his jaw shut, holding back any impulsive words. "Listen, Tim. I may be young west of the Pecos, but I'm not inexperienced. I can see ahead. No matter how strong these rustlers are, how hidden their work, or how involved they are with supposedly honest men, they can't last forever."

"They've been around since the pioneers came," Morton countered. "And they'll keep going as long as there's a single steer left."

"Well, if you're gonna look at it like that, I'm just gonna assume you're one of them rustlers!" Morton's face twisted with anger, and for a moment, I thought he was gonna hit me with his whip. But then, he seemed to realize how foolish he was being and let out a booming laugh.

"It ain't funny," I continued. "If you're gonna act like a coward, what else am I supposed to think?"

"Act like a coward?" Morton repeated, clearly offended. "You can't fool me, kid. I know real men when I see 'em. Ain't no difference between the men here in Pecos and anywhere else. If you act like you're scared, it's just an act. You've got nerve, I can tell."

I nodded, feeling a sense of pride at Morton's words. "That's right. And if you think these rustlers are gonna keep me from going into business with a rancher, you're dead wrong. We need some fresh blood out here, some young guns like me to get things going again."

Morton seemed to consider my words for a moment, looking like a storm cloud was brewing inside him. I could tell he was a tough old cowboy, one who had probably seen his fair share of trouble.

"Well, I reckon you might be right," he finally said. "I'll look you up next time I'm in town, Tim."

With that, we parted ways, and I made my way back down the street to the Hope So saloon, feeling more confident than ever.

As I walked in, I knew the tasks ahead of me were sincere, but displeasing. I had to mix with a low, profane set, and cultivate them. I had to drink occasionally despite my deftness at emptying glasses on the floor and gamble with them and strangers. I had to play the part of a flush and flashy cowboy, half drunk, always ready to laugh or fight. It was the night of the fifth day after Foster's departure when I went to the rendezvous we maintained at the pile of rocks out in the open. The night was clear, bright starlight without any moon, making it safer to be abroad. From my covert, I had often seen dark figures skulking in and out of Linrock. It would have been interesting to hold up these mysterious travelers, but that had not been our game. I had enough to keep my own tracks hidden and my own comings and goings. I liked to be out in the night, with the darkness close down to the earth, and the feeling of a limitless open all around. I listened for Foster's soft step, but also for any sound, like the yelp of coyote or mourn of wolf, the creak of wind in the dead brush, the distant clatter of hoofs, or a woman's singing voice faint from the town. Just when I was about to give up for that evening, Foster came looming like a black giant long before I heard his soft step. It was good to feel his grip, even if it hurt, because after five days I had begun to worry.

"Well, old boy, how's tricks?" he asked easily.

"Well, old man, did you land that son of a gun in jail?" I replied.

"You bet I did. And he'll stay there for a while. Del Rio rather liked the idea, Tim. All right there. I side-stepped Sanderson on the way back. But over here at the little village Barkley they call it, I was held up."

"I couldn't help it, man. There wasn't no road to take," I explained to my partner.

"Held up?" he asked.

"Yeah, the buckboard got held up. I managed to get into the brush just in time. They started shooting too soon," I replied.

"Did you get any of them?" he inquired.

"I didn't stick around to find out," I chuckled. "Had to hoof it to Linrock, and it's a long walk."

"Have you been to your place tonight?" he questioned.

"I snuck in the back. Had to make sure no one was waiting for me in the dark," I responded.

"You need to find a safer spot. Why not sleep out in the open every night?" he suggested.

"Sure, that's fine on a trail, but I need food and a few comforts. I'll risk the dobe for a little while longer," I explained.

I recounted everything I had seen and done during his absence, holding back one thing. What I did tell him sobered him up, bringing a quiet and thoughtful mood.

"That's all pertaining to our job, Vaughn," my partner replied. "The rest is just sentiment. I had a thing for that little Langdon girl, but we quarreled. It's over now, and it's probably for the best."

"Did you really care for her?" I asked.

"I'm afraid so. It hurts, but a love affair could have made me soft and hindered me. I'm glad it's over," he said.

He didn't say anything else, but the pressure of his hand on my knee showed his sympathy. I continued, "The other thing concerns you. Remember how I overheard Darling talking bad about you to Miss Barkley? He swore you'd never come back. After he left, Miss Barkley felt bad about what he said. She thought he meant you would be killed."

The conversation ended there, and we went about our business.

She said she would be happy if someone killed you, but she couldn't bring herself to actually want it. She called you a bloody ruffian, yet she didn't think you deserved to be shot. "She talked about the difference between your terrible character and your impressive stature. She called you a magnificent fellow, that's what she did. Then she got choked up and told Gwen something in shame and disgrace."

"What shame and disgrace?" asked Foster, clearly intrigued. "What did she say?"

"She admitted that she was taken with you and even had a little dream about you. And she hated herself for it."

I'll never forget the look in Vaughn Foster's eyes. It didn't matter that it was dark; I could see the fixed gleam, then the leaping, shadowy light. "Did she really say that?" His voice was unsteady. "Amazing! Even if it only lasted a minute! Maybe we could- we could- If it wasn't for this awful job! Tim, have you realized yet what I have to do to Diane Barkley?"

"Yes," I replied. "Vaughn, you haven't fallen for her, have you?"

I couldn't interpret the terrible emotion in his eyes as anything else. He didn't answer me at all, and I thought he was going to break my arm with how tightly he was holding it. "You said you know what I have to do to Diane Barkley," he said hoarsely.

"Yes, you have to ruin her happiness, if not her life."

"Why? Speak up, Tim. This is like a punch in the gut. For a moment, I thought you had a different plan than me. No hope. Ruin her life! Why?"

I couldn't explain Foster's intense distress any other way than that the realization had brought him sharp pain that was both incomprehensible and agonizing. I couldn't tell if it was because he suddenly realized he loved Diane Barkley or if it was because he was convinced he was fated to destroy her. But I did know that he needed to tell the brutal truth.

"Dang it, Foster, you're gonna ruin Diane Barkley. If you can't arrest her father, you're gonna have to kill him," I warned him.

"Why in God's name would I need to do that?" Foster demanded.

"Because Barkley's the leader of the Linrock gang of rustlers," I explained.

After that conversation, we talked about our plan of action. I urged Foster to be vigilant, to be prepared for any attack. I told him that if he got shot in a fair fight, that was just part of the job. But he couldn't let himself be ambushed or killed in his sleep. He promised me he wouldn't, but I could hear the desperation in his voice.

We decided that I would work on gaining the trust of Dempsey and Morton, and then Zimmer and other ranchers who could help us. We needed to find clues to the rustler gang's guilt, and we needed a group of deputies to fight with us when the time came.

Foster would be the center of attention in Linrock, so we agreed that he needed to be bold and show his nerve. The more he stood up to the rustlers, the less likely they were to ambush him. But we needed a jail to hold them once we caught them.

After arresting prisoners, it was crucial to keep them contained, otherwise all the effort would be pointless. Using an adobe house as a jail was not an option as it could easily be cut or torn down. It took some brainstorming, but I recalled an old stone house at the end of the main street, which had been abandoned for some time. Foster agreed to rent it and hire guards to watch over and feed the prisoners. Even if they managed to escape, it wouldn't damage the principles we stood for.

Foster and I both had a strong feeling that Barkley was guilty, but we needed proof. Our experience in detecting and sensing hidden guilt had sharpened our senses. Foster had made some mistakes in the past, but I had never made a single one. However, having conviction was one thing, and having proof was another. Once we had enough evidence, we faced the daunting task of capturing desperate men who were in control of a wild country. It was a challenge, but we were ready to tackle it with patience and determination.

Foster and I had different motivations, but we both shared a common goal of saving the Ranger Service. Foster was passionate about upholding the law in Texas and making life safer and happier for honest pioneers. I, on the other hand, was driven by the excitement, danger, and mental challenge of the job. While I also wanted to help those in need, it was the thrill of the game that kept me going.

The next morning, I rode with the young ladies. Gwen's advances were persistent and obvious, but I pretended not to notice. I knew that my hard-earned self-control was in danger of slipping away. Despite this, I remained attentive and respectful, ensuring the safety of my charges. However, the carefree cowboy that I once was seemed to be a distant memory.

Gwen, being the typical woman, showed some remorse for her behavior. But my indifference only fueled her desire to win me back. She was the type to value what she had lost and would do anything to regain it. I saw an opportunity for revenge, even though she had been kind to me. I couldn't forget the snide comment she made about being kissed by her admirers. Sentiment aside, I couldn't make amends with her.

We stopped on a ridge to rest, and I found a shady spot under a mesquite tree. The girls wandered off, and I nearly dozed off. Suddenly, I heard footsteps and rustling. Then, I felt a soft thud behind me, and I jumped. It was Gwen's little hands on my shoulders, and her fragrant hair brushed against my cheek. She whispered, "Tim, don't you love me anymore?"

Chapter Four.

That evening, I caught sight of Foster at our designated spot, and we exchanged information and mulled over the intricacies of our predicament.

The stone house had been rented by Foster to serve as a jail. The blacksmith was tasked with fitting a door and window that could withstand any attack. The townsfolk, including idlers and strangers, flocked to see the spectacle. It was a significant event for Linrock. Foster announced that he needed to hire a jailer and a guard. The sarcastic humor of the townsfolk made it clear that they were keen on filling these positions. Foster and I were about to part ways when I remembered Miss Barkley's upcoming party. I informed Foster, but he shook his head in doubt. Could Barkley really be a shrewd and cunning leader of cattle rustlers and still maintain his daughter's innocence and hold parties for the very people he had robbed? It was a notion that only merciless Rangers could believe.

Thursday evening arrived, and it was clear that the girls had different attitudes towards the party. Gwen aimed to outshine all the other young ladies and attract all the young men. Miss Barkley, on the other hand, wanted to open her father's home to the people of Linrock, to show that she could bring happiness and entertainment to what had been a long and cheerless abode. I was in the parlor carrying flowers for decoration when Miss Barkley received word that her father had ridden off with three unidentified horsemen. She was disappointed, but it was clear that the news had a deeper impact on her. I overheard Dick's remark about the colonel's haste, and it left me pondering.

Barkley was known for his spontaneous rides, but this particular event was different. The house was lit up with every lantern and lamp available, and the cowboys arrived in their best attire, eager for the festivities to begin. Townspeople, both young and old, soon followed. Miss Barkley welcomed them all and explained her father's absence. The music was provided by two cowboys with banjos and an elderly man with a fiddle, and though it wasn't perfect, it was enough to get everyone dancing.

As I moved from the porch to the parlor to the patio, I couldn't help but be amused by the scene before me. The bright dresses and flashy scarfs of the cowboys, along with the beautiful flowers and decorations, made for a lively and colorful atmosphere. During the dance, the sound of boots shuffling on the floor was constant, and during the breaks, there was a low hum of chatter and laughter.

Although I wasn't one to usually wander around, my eyes were fixed on Gwen Langdon. She was wearing a white dress with a low neckline and short sleeves, and she looked absolutely stunning. I couldn't help but feel jealous as she seemed to make sure I saw her every chance she got. Despite my jealousy, I couldn't help but be mesmerized by her beauty.

As I strolled around the promenade, I noticed her arm in the embrace of some proud cowboy or gallant young buck from town. She would give them a languishing glance that probably did as much damage to them as it did to me. One day, she caught me red-handed in my pursuit of her and then, whether by intent or from indifference, she stopped paying me any attention. However, I noticed that from that moment on, her gaiety gradually transformed into coquettishness and soon into flirtation. Curious to see how far she would go, I followed her shamelessly everywhere she went, even to the waltz. To her credit, she always backed off when some young fellow tried to take things too far. Young Waters was the only one successful enough to kiss her, and there was more strength in his conquest of her than any decent fellow could be proud of.

When Reuben Darling sought Gwen out, my jealousy was mixed with real anxiety. I had bumped into Darling several times that evening. He wasn't drunk, yet he was under the influence of liquor. I believed that Gwen wouldn't have walked with him had she known, given her abhorrence of drink. Anyway, I followed them, staying close to the shadows. Darling was unusually happy, and I saw him put his arm around her without any remonstrance. When the music resumed, they went back to the house, and Darling danced with Gwen, not ungracefully for a man who rode horses as much as he did. After the dance, he waved aside Gwen's many partners, not as gaily as would have been consistent with good feeling, and led her away. I followed them.

They ended their walk at the far end of the patio, where a small arbor had been built among the flowers and vines, lit up by brightly colored lights. Gwen's energy seemed to have diminished. As soon as they were out of my view, I heard Gwen cry out, not in alarm but in frustration. I took it as an opportunity and quickly ran back towards them, my hand on my gun. When I arrived at the arbor, I saw that Darling had been holding Gwen, but he released her when he heard me. Gwen's face turned white, and she put her hand over her chest, thinking I was going to harm Darling.

I apologized, explaining that I had heard a noise and thought someone was in danger. I made an excuse for my behavior, stating that Miss Barkley had given me instructions to keep an eye out for accidents and fires. As I stepped away, to my surprise, Gwen apologized to Darling and then rushed over to me. She grabbed my arm, saying it was time for our dance. She whispered to me that she was afraid of Darling and that I had scared her as well, but I reassured her that I had only been trying to keep her safe.

As we walked through the patio, Gwen told me that she thought of me whenever she was frightened since we arrived. She said that she felt safe with me nearby. We stopped at the entrance to the big parlor, and Gwen stood in front of me, looking down with a flushed face. She twisted a silver button on my vest as she spoke, and I could barely hear her over the sound of the passing couples. Gwen looked as sweet as ever, and I couldn't help but feel a twinge of affection towards her.

"Let's dance," she said, grabbing my arm. "Reuben chased off my partner. I'm happy for the opportunity. Dance with me, Tim, not because I asked, but because you want to. If not, don't bother."

I couldn't handle much more of this. It was unlikely that I would have another evening like this, at least not in this area. I reluctantly agreed, and we entered the parlor. Amid all the chaos, she whispered, "I've been terrible to you."

The dance felt like it lasted only a moment. She was light and graceful, glowing and attractive, floating near me with our hands clasped. Then the music stopped, the couples found seats, and Gwen and I were approached by Miss Barkley. She complimented us on our graceful dancing, and Gwen mentioned how she didn't have to reach up too far to dance with me. I was speechless for once and said nothing. Darling had returned and was now standing in the doorway, cigarette in his mouth, leading to the patio. At the same time, I heard heavy boots stomping on the porch, and Darling's expression changed from surprise to fear. I turned around to see Vaughn Foster leaning his head to enter from the other side. The dancers backed away, and at the sight of him, I was once again the Ranger, his ally. Foster was pale and sweating, without a hat, his coat turned up, and he held the lapels together with his left hand. In the ensuing silence, Miss Barkley stood up, white as her dress. The other young women gawked in amazement, and their partners were excited.

"Miss Barkley, I came to search your house!" Foster gasped, politely but firmly.

I released my hands from Gwen's grip and stepped forward, leaving the corner. Foster was running towards us, his coat clutched tightly to his chest. I felt a sense of anticipation, knowing that something was about to happen. Miss Barkley's expression went from surprise to anger, which she struggled to control. "As my father is not here, I am in charge and I will not allow you to search my house," she declared.

Foster responded sternly, "I regret to say that I must search your house without your permission." Miss Barkley was not pleased with this response. She stood tall, her chest heaving, her eyes blazing with anger. "How dare you intrude here? You have already insulted us enough. To search my house tonight, to disrupt my party, is worse than an outrage! Why would you want to search here? Is it for the same reason you brought an innocent man into my father's court? I forbid you to take another step into this house."

Foster's face turned pale, and I wondered if it was because of her scorn or something he was hiding under his coat. "Miss Barkley, I do not require a warrant to search houses," he said. "However, I will respect your command this time. It would be a shame to spoil your party. Let me add, perhaps you misunderstand me. I was shot by a rustler and he fled. I chased him here, and he has taken refuge in your father's house. He is hiding somewhere."

Foster opened his coat, revealing a light-colored shirt that was stained with blood. Drops of dark red fell to the floor. "Oh!" cried Miss Barkley. Her anger dissipated, replaced by horror and pity as she imagined that Foster was mortally wounded. It was a gruesome sight, one that no woman should have to witness.

"I can handle this. I'll find the rustler and make sure he's dealt with properly. Miss Barkley trusts me to handle this without violence, and I won't let her down." As I spoke, I could feel my anger simmering just beneath the surface. Reuben Darling had no right to question my abilities or my intentions.

Gwen clung to my arm, her eyes wide with fear and excitement. "Be careful, Tim," she whispered. "I don't want anything to happen to you."

I smiled down at her, my heart racing with adrenaline. "Don't worry, Gwen. I've got this." And with that, I pushed open the door and stepped out into the night.

The air was cold and crisp, the stars shining brightly overhead. I could hear the distant sound of a guitar and the laughter of the dancers inside, but outside it was quiet and still. I took a deep breath and set off towards the edge of town, my eyes scanning the darkness for any sign of movement.

It didn't take long for me to spot something. A shadow moving along the ground, just beyond the edge of the streetlights. I froze, my hand going to my gun, and watched as the figure darted behind a nearby building.

I crept forward, my heart pounding in my chest, and peered around the corner. There, huddled in the shadows, was a man. He was young, with a scruffy beard and a wild look in his eyes.

"Hey!" I called out, stepping forward. "What are you doing here?"

The man spun around, his hand going to his own gun. "None of your damn business," he snarled.

I didn't hesitate. I drew my own gun and aimed it at him. "I think it is my business. You just shot a man, and I'm here to make sure you pay for it."

The man hesitated, his eyes flickering nervously between me and the gun. "You don't understand," he said finally. "I had no choice. Foster was going to ruin everything."

I frowned, lowering my gun slightly. "What do you mean? What were you trying to protect?"

The man hesitated for a moment, then seemed to make up his mind. "I can't tell you," he said. "But I can promise you this. If you let me go, I'll make it worth your while."

I shook my head. "I'm sorry. I can't do that. You're coming with me."

And with that, I stepped forward and grabbed the man by the arm. He struggled for a moment, then seemed to give up, letting me lead him back towards town. I could hear the distant sound of shouting and gunfire, but I didn't let it distract me. I had a job to do, and I was going to see it through.

"But I ain't tellin' you nothin'. You can't prove nothin' anyway." I tightened my grip on his collar, feeling my patience wearing thin. "Listen, kid, you've been rustlin' cattle from Miss Barkley's ranch. You can either come clean or face the consequences." He hesitated for a moment, then seemed to come to a decision. "Alright, alright.

I did it. But I had to. My dad's sick, and we needed the money." I nodded, understanding his predicament, but also knowing that the law had to be upheld. "Well, you're comin' with us. We'll let the sheriff sort this out." We led him outside, where Miss Barkley and the other cowboys were waiting anxiously. "We found him," I announced, and handed Bo over to the sheriff, who had just arrived. As they rode off, I couldn't help but feel a sense of satisfaction. Another rustler caught, another job well done.

"I figured Barkley's was the safest place around," I said confidently. My companions didn't seem convinced, but they didn't know the full extent of the danger I was facing. The image of Foster's bloody chest was still fresh in my mind, and I knew I had to be careful. I couldn't reveal my true feelings or show any unusual interest in Foster, not now.

When Snecker was finally captured, I played it cool and asked what Darling planned to do with him. I let Snecker go and put my weapon away. Snecker seemed relieved, and I guessed he didn't fancy the sight of a cocked gun pointed in his direction. Darling took charge and pushed Snecker into the hall.

I followed them out to the back of the house and then hurried back to Miss Barkley and Gwen. They were still shaken up, but I reassured them that there wouldn't be any more trouble. Miss Barkley was curious about the rustler's identity, and I tried to deflect suspicion by suggesting he had just been looking for a place to hide.

She asked if her father would have arrested him, and I replied honestly that he might have made things difficult for him. Suddenly, Miss Barkley remembered the presence of the Ranger and exclaimed in surprise.

The sight was gruesome, blood covering the man's entire front. "How is he still standing?" I asked Tim. "Do you think it'll kill him?"

"Hard to say. Foster's a tough one," Tim replied.

"Please, Tim, go find him. See how he's doing," she pleaded.

Glad for the chance to help, I hurried down towards town. As I approached his little adobe house, I made sure to be cautious and not draw any attention. I whistled low, a signal he'd recognize, and he opened the door for me.

"Hello, son," he greeted me. "You needn't have worried. Sling a blanket over that window so no one can see in."

Foster had his shirt off and was bandaging a bullet wound on his shoulder. "Let me tie that up," I offered, taking the strips of linen.

"Ahuh! Shot you from behind, didn't he?" Foster asked.

"How else, you crazy lady-charmer? It's a wonder I didn't have to tell you that."

He recounted the circumstances of the shooting, which weren't much different from previous attempts on his life. "Snecker's a good runner if he's not a good shot," Foster concluded. I finished bandaging his wound and couldn't help but admire his strong shoulders. I noticed several scars on his skin from previous bullet wounds. I had the impression that his strength and vitality were unconquerable.

"You knew it was Bill Snecker's son?" I asked, telling him about finding the rustler.

"Sure. Jim Dempsey pointed him out to me yesterday. Both Sneckers are in town. We're going to be busy from now on, Tim," Foster said.

"It can't come soon enough for me," I replied. "Should I quit my job and come out from behind these cowboy togs?"

"Not yet. We need proof, Tim. We've got to be able to prove things."

"Let's stay at the ranch a bit longer," I suggested.

Bo Snecker was clearly terrified until he recognized Darling. "Doesn't that prove something?" he asked.

"No, that's not enough. We need to catch Barkley and Darling in the act," I replied.

"I don't like the idea of you going alone," I protested. "Remember what Neal told me. It's time for me to stay close with a couple of guns. You'll never have to use one."

"The hell I won't," Foster retorted, his passion evident. I was surprised that my comment had angered him. "You're all wrong. I know when to use a gun. Rangers have a reputation for being trigger-happy, and unfortunately, it's probably accurate."

"Did you shoot at Snecker?" I asked.

"I could have shot him in the back, but that wasn't the right way to do it. I aimed at his legs, trying to bring him down. I would have made him tell us everything he knew, but he was too quick for me."

"Shooting at his legs? No wonder he ran. He knew what you were up to. It's funny how these rustlers and gunmen don't mind being killed, but being crippled, roped, and jailed is a fate worse than death for them. So, am I supposed to continue falling in love with that sweet girl up at the ranch instead of facing things with you?"

Foster chuckled, but he also took my concerns seriously. "Tim, you think you're patient, but you don't know what patience really is. I won't rush this job. But I have an idea. I'll stay hidden most of the time when you're not around. That's doable. I'll keep an eye out for you when you're in town. We'll go to the same places. And if I get busy, you can follow me discreetly. Does that work for you?"

"Perfect," I replied, relieved that we had come to an agreement.

"Well, I gotta head back to tell Miss Barkley that you're alright," I said to Foster. He was finishing up putting on a clean shirt, being careful not to disrupt the bandages. He stopped and turned to face me with a desperate look. "Tim, did she show any sympathy?" he asked eagerly.

"She was really upset about it. She thought you were gonna die," I replied.

"Did she send you?" he asked.

"Yep. And she said to hurry," I said, feeling a bit smug about the possibility of Foster having feelings for her too.

"Do you think she would have cared if I was hurt bad?" Foster asked, sounding like a nervous kid with a blush on his face.

"Care? Vaughn, you're as dense as you say I'm crazy. Diane Barkley's fallen in love with you! That's it. Love at first sight. She doesn't know it, but I do," I said confidently.

Foster stood there, looking like he'd been hit by a bullet straight to the heart. Maybe my words were too much, but I believed them. "Tim, for God's sake! That's a terrible thing to say!" he exclaimed.

"No, it's not terrible to say. It's just a terrible fact," I said. "I could be wrong, but I swear I'm right. When you opened your coat and showed your bloody chest, I'll never forget the look in her eyes. She was furious, filled with hate. Then something beautiful broke through. Pity, fear, and agony at the thought of your death. If that's not love, then I don't know what is. She thinks she hates you, but she really loves you."

"Get out of here," Foster ordered, his voice thick. I left, but not before taking a quick peek out the door and listening for a moment. Then I hurried back towards the ranch.

The stars shone bright and big, so calm and cold that it hurt to look at them. It made me wonder about the fate of Vaughn Foster and me. Bitterness, an emotion rare for me, crept in. Most Rangers let go of love when they joined the Service and rarely found it again. But love had found me, and I knew that Vaughn was in the same boat. The adventurer in me stirred as I marveled at the situation. We had fallen into a tangle of circumstances that Rangers were not prepared for. I left with regret, remorse, and sorrow in my heart, but also with the excitement of the game tingling through me.

I returned to the ranch, feeling mischievous. I wanted to plant the same seed in Diane Barkley's heart that I had in Foster's. Perhaps it was a strange foreshadowing of a coming event, or maybe it was just my love for mischief. I hoped that if Diane loved, the event might be less tragic. Love could save us all. That was the shadowy thought flitting through my mind.

As I arrived at the ranch, dancing had resumed, and Miss Barkley was looking for me. She searched my face with her eyes, silencing my last qualm of conscience. "Let's go to the patio," I suggested. "I don't want anyone to overhear us."

Outside, under the starry sky, Diane looked beautiful, her skin glowing white. I sensed her trembling, and my heart sank. Perhaps my gravity presaged the worst.

Vaughn had been shot in the shoulder, but it wasn't a serious injury. I went to his humble abode and he was surprised to see me. I bandaged his wound and he was grateful. He confided in me that he had no friends, which made me feel sorry for him. When I relayed the story to Miss Barkley, she expressed sympathy for Vaughn and said that my words may have hurt him more than the bullet. I agreed with her and told her that Foster had been wronged. I knew his record along the Rio Grande and it wasn't fair to judge him without knowing the truth. Miss Barkley was confused and asked me what she should do. I urged her to think things through for herself and not to just rely on what her father and cousin Reuben told her. She was struggling to make sense of life out here and her father's strange behavior. Despite only seeing him twice a year since she was a little girl, she was still trying to understand him.

He's a man of two faces. When I see that other side of him, the one I never knew existed, he's like a stranger to me. "I want to be a good daughter and help him fight his battles, but he doesn't satisfy me. He's grown impatient and wants me to go back to Louisiana. It's all so mysterious," she confided in me.

"You're right," I agreed, feeling for her. "It's all a mystery and trouble for you. Maybe it's best if you go home."

"Are you suggesting I leave my father?" she asked, her tone defensive.

"I am," I advised. "You've come at a troublesome time. You can always return later if-"

"Never. I came to stay, and I'll stay," she interrupted, her temper flaring.

"Miss Barkley," I began again, taking a deep breath. "I should tell you something about Foster."

"Go on," she urged.

"Doesn't he seem like the furthest thing from a brutal Ranger now?" I asked.

"He was at least a gentleman," she admitted.

"Rangers don't let anything get in the way of their duty. He was courteous to you even after you insulted him. He respected your wishes and didn't break up the dance. This may not seem like a big deal, but Foster was actually chasing an outlaw who had shot him. Under normal circumstances, he would have searched your house like a lion tearing through its prey to find that rustler."

"But he didn't," she realized.

"No, he didn't. And I think you should know why," I said, hesitating for a moment before continuing. "I believe it's because of you."

"Because of me?" she asked, her eyes shining with emotion.

"Yes, because of you," I confirmed. "I think he felt something for you, something that made him hesitate. Something that made him see you as more than just a suspect."

"What are you saying?" she asked, her voice barely above a whisper.

"I'm saying that he might have feelings for you," I revealed, knowing that I was about to change the course of her life forever.

My throat constricted, making it difficult to speak. "He's fallen for you," I managed to say in a raspy voice. "Love at first sight! It's a terrible thing. Hopeless, really. I saw it, I felt it. I can't explain how, but I just know."

"That's why he's holding back," I continued. "He's on your side. He's alone in this difficult task, with everyone against him. If he fails, you might be the reason. You should be kinder in your thoughts towards him, and wait before you judge him further."

"If he survives, time will prove him to be noble instead of vile. If he doesn't, which is likely, you'll feel better for giving him the benefit of the doubt. He loved you."

She stood there, momentarily blinded by my words. Then, with her hands clasped to her chest, she walked straight into the darkness of her room.

Chapter Five.

"He asked, wiping his hands on his apron. "Haven't seen you in a while." "Just taking a little ride," I replied. "Well, you picked a good day for it," he said, nodding at the clear blue sky. I stepped inside the restaurant and ordered breakfast. As I ate, I couldn't help but think about Miss Barkley and our conversation the night before. She had a way of getting under my skin, making me question things I had always taken for granted. After breakfast, I walked out onto the street and watched as people went about their business. The town had a certain charm to it, despite its rough edges. I couldn't help but feel a sense of nostalgia as I looked at the old buildings and the men lounging on the corners. As I made my way back to the ranch, I couldn't shake the feeling that something was off. I had been a Ranger for a long time, and I had seen my fair share of violence and bloodshed. But Miss Barkley had made me question whether there was more to life than just fighting and killing. I arrived back at the ranch just as the sun was setting. The young ladies were still nowhere to be seen, and I knew I had a long night ahead of me. But for the first time in a long time, I felt like I was seeing the world with fresh eyes. Maybe there was more to life than just being a Ranger. Maybe there was something else out there, something worth fighting for.

Morton was really eager to see you. I convinced him to not go up to Barkley's. What kind of game were you playing with Frank?" "Jim, I just wanted to make sure he was a trustworthy rancher before making a stock deal with him," I replied. "He says you told him he wasn't a rustler and had no yellow streak. Frank can't get over those two hunches. When he sees you he's going to swear he's no rustler, but he does have a yellow streak, unless..." This Texan had eyes like flint striking fire. "Unless?" I asked sharply. Jim took a deep breath and looked around the room before speaking again. "Well," he replied in a low voice, "Me and Frank think you've picked the right men. It was me who sent those letters to the Ranger captain in Austin. So who in hell are you?" It was my turn to take a deep breath. It had taken me six weeks to gain the trust of this Texan who I instinctively felt had been affected by the corruption that plagued Linrock. There was no one else in the room, and I reached into the inside pocket of my buckskin vest and turned the lining out. A bright, silver object in the shape of a star flashed as I put it, pocket and all, under Jim's hard gaze. He couldn't help but see it; United States Deputy Marshall. "By golly," he whispered, hitting the table with his fist. "Tim, you sure rang true to me. But never as a cowboy!" "Jim, there are a lot of us around!" Heavy footsteps could be heard on the walk outside. Soon, Foster's large figure appeared in the doorway. "Hello," I greeted. "Foster, meet Jim Dempsey." "Hello," Foster replied slowly. "I think I know Dempsey." "Not this one," I said. "He's the old Dempsey. He used to own the Hope So saloon. It was legitimate when he ran it. Maybe he'll get it back soon."

I couldn't help but chuckle at my terrible pun. Foster stood next to me, his sharp gaze fixed on the man I had just introduced. Dempsey, in a split second, connected the dots and realized the connection between me and the Ranger. He seemed to be on the verge of passing out, perhaps from shock, hope, or fear. "Foster, do you know who's in charge of the rustlers around here?" Foster didn't beat around the bush, as was typical of him. His voice was deep, calm, and collected, which seemed to soothe Dempsey. "No," Dempsey replied. "Does anyone know?" Foster pressed on. "Well, I reckon there's not a single honest person in Pecos who knows," Dempsey answered confidently. "But you have your suspicions?" "We do." "You can keep your suspicions to yourself. But what do you think about the group of regulars who hang around the saloons?" "They're just a bad bunch," Dempsey replied with ease. "Most of them have been here for years, while others come and go. Some of them work odd jobs, rustle a few cows, steal, or rob to make some quick cash for gambling and drinking. They're just a bad bunch." "But what about the strangers who come and go without getting acquainted?" Foster prodded. "Some of them could be rustlers. Bill and Bo Snecker are in town right now. Bill's a known cattle thief, and Bo's no good. He's got the makings of a gunfighter." "They could be rustlers, but the kid doesn't seem careful enough for this gang," Dempsey said thoughtfully. "Then there's Jack Blome. He comes to town often and lives up in the hills. He always has three or four strangers with him. Blome's a fancy gunfighter. He shot a gambler here last fall and got into a fight in Sanderson recently, taking down two cowboys. Blome's killed a dozen Pecos men. He's a rustler, too, but I don't think he's the brains behind the secret outfit, if he's even in it at all." Foster seemed pleased with Dempsey's insights.

Foster and Dempsey were in a serious conversation about the strange and deadly hold on their community. Rustling cattle was one thing, but the cold-blooded murder of anyone who spoke out was too much for them to bear. Foster was determined to put an end to it, and Dempsey's renewed spirit was a sign that he wasn't alone in his thinking. Suddenly, the sound of hooves interrupted them and Foster gestured for the narrator to hide behind a curtain. They watched as Reuben Darling and a red-headed cowboy named Brick entered the store. Darling seemed surprised to see the Ranger and gave him a hard look before addressing Foster. "That was the second break of yours last night," he accused.

"If you come around the ranch again with that kind of talk, you'll regret it," warned Darling. It was strange that a man who had lived in the west for ten years couldn't see something in Foster that forbade that kind of behavior. It wasn't courage that Darling showed; brave men were rarely intolerant. Foster, with his matchless nerve and cool, unobtrusive manner, was certainly courteous and almost gentle in his speech. Darling, on the other hand, was a hot-headed Louisianian of French extraction who had never been crossed in anything. He was strong, brutal, and passionate, which made him a fool in this situation.

I hated this smooth, dark-skinned Southerner, and the way Foster looked at him brought joy to me. But Foster remained silent in response to Darling's affront. "I think you used your Ranger bluff just to get near Diane Barkley," sneered Darling. "If you come up there again, there'll be hell!"

"You're damn right there'll be hell!" retorted Foster, his voice ringing high. I saw his face turn thick, dark red. Had Darling's mention of Diane Barkley been motivated by jealousy or love? It had clearly pierced into the depths of Foster, perhaps more than any other insult could have. "Diane Barkley wouldn't stoop to know a dirty blood-tracker like you," said Darling hotly. He wasn't intentionally trying to rouse Foster; the man was simply rancorous. "You're a cheap bluffer, a four-flush, a damned interfering conceited Ranger!"

Long before Darling finished his tirade, Foster's face had lost its color. The cool shade, steady eyes like ice on fire, and ruthless lips warned me, if not Darling, that Foster was not to be trifled with. "Darling, I won't take offense because you seem to be championing your beautiful cousin," replied Foster, his speech slow and biting.

"Let me return the compliment, you're a fine Southerner! Why, you're nothing more than a cheap, two-faced rustler," Foster spat out the words. Darling's face contorted in anger, and he made a move for his gun. But Foster was quicker. With lightning speed, he lunged forward and knocked Darling backwards, causing him to crash into a table and chairs before landing hard against the wall.

"Don't even think about it," Foster warned as Darling struggled to get back up. "Get away from your gun!" Brick yelled, trying to diffuse the situation. But Darling was beyond reason. His face twisted with rage, he reached for his hip, his fingers itching to draw.

Without hesitation, Foster fired his gun, hitting Darling square in the arm. Darling's gun clattered to the ground as he screamed in agony. Blood spattered the tablecloths as he thrashed around in pain. Brick quickly dragged him out of the establishment, leaving the horses behind.

Foster calmly sheathed his gun, seemingly unfazed by the violence that had just occurred. "Well, I guess that opens the ball," he said as he walked out of the building. Dempsey, on the other hand, seemed fascinated by the blood stains on the tablecloths, rubbing his hands over them like a ghoul.

"What did you shoot him for?" Dempsey asked, his voice shaking with fear. "He was drawing on you. Shooting the arms off men like him won't do out here."

I couldn't help but agree with Dempsey. "That bull-headed fool will only attract attention to himself and his gang. He's just the man I've been waiting for. Besides, shooting him would have been murder."

"Murder!" exclaimed Dempsey in disbelief. Foster just chuckled in response. "We've just had a few pleasant moments with the man who has made it healthy to keep close-mouthed in Linrock," he said with a smirk.

"He's a fool, and slow at that. Should I kill him when I don't have to?" I asked, contemplating the situation.

"It would have been the trick," Jim replied confidently. "I'm not considering whether he's really a rustler or not. It just won't work, because these guys out here won't be afraid of you."

"Listen, Dempsey. If a man is going to be afraid of me at all, that trick will make him more afraid of me. I know it. It works out. When Darling cools down he'll remember, he'll start thinking, he'll realize that I could have killed him instead of risking a shot at his arm. I bet he'll go pale next time he sees me."

"That might be true, Foster. But if Darling is the man you think he is, he'll start that secret underground business. It's been pretty healthy these last six months. You can bet on it. If that secret work does start, you'll have more reason to suspect Darling. I won't feel very safe from now on. I heard you call him a rustler. He knows that. Why, Darling won't be able to sleep at night now. He and Barkley have always been after me."

"Dempsey, what do your eyes do?" Foster asked. "Be careful. And now, go see your friend Morton. Tell him this game is getting hot. Together you approach four or five men you know well and can absolutely trust. Hey, someone's coming. Meet Tim and me tonight, out in the open, a quarter of a mile straight from the end of this street. You'll find a pile of stones. Meet us there tonight at ten o'clock."

For the next few days, whenever I was in town, I kept a close eye on Foster or made sure he was safe under cover. Nothing happened.

Whenever he received a letter, he would announce it to the entire saloon. The men would gather around him, eagerly asking who it was from and what it said. It was during one of these announcements that Foster and I overheard something that made our blood run cold.

Roberts had received a letter addressed to "Jack Blome" and it was postmarked from a town called "Sneckerville." Suddenly, everything made sense. The Sneckers had gone into hiding because they knew that Blome was coming for them. And now, it seemed that he had arrived.

Foster and I exchanged a worried glance. Blome was a notorious outlaw, feared by everyone in the area. If he was in town, it meant trouble. We knew that we had to act fast.

But before we could do anything, a commotion erupted outside. We rushed to the window to see what was happening. A group of men on horses had just ridden into town. They were heavily armed and wore bandanas over their faces. It was clear that they were up to no good.

Foster and I quickly grabbed our guns and headed outside. We were the only lawmen in town and it was our duty to protect the innocent. As we stepped out into the street, we were confronted by the gang of outlaws.

"Get out of our way, Ranger," one of them snarled.

But Foster stood his ground. "Not a chance, boys. You're not welcome here."

The outlaws laughed and raised their guns. It was clear that they meant business. Foster and I exchanged a determined look and prepared for the fight of our lives.

Whenever the stage arrived in town, a crowd would gather at the old man's store, bringing in a good amount of revenue. But one night, after the crowd had dispersed, two thugs barged into the store, beat up the old man, and robbed him. The old man didn't say anything about it, but when Foster came by, he reluctantly gave a description of his attackers and their names. Foster immediately went in search of the men and found them at Lerett's place. I happened to be there when it all went down.

Foster walked up to a table where Sim Bass and a group of men were sitting. He tapped Bass on the shoulder and said, "Get up, I want you." Bass looked up, but before he could say anything, Foster grabbed him by the collar and sent him sliding, chair and all, into the bar. Bass was left lying there, wondering what hit him. Foster then turned to Miller and said, "I want you. Get up." Miller complied and Foster kicked Bass to make sure he was still conscious. Foster searched both men in front of their comrades, took their money and weapons, and marched them out, followed by a growing crowd.

Foster took the two men to Roberts' store, where they were identified and the stolen money was returned. Then, Foster marched them down to his stone jail and locked them up. The crowd that had gathered found the whole thing highly entertaining, cracking jokes about Bass and Miller. Even after the two were locked up, the jokes continued, directed at Foster's jailer and guard, who looked just as disreputable as the prisoners. The seriousness of the incident was completely lost on the audience.

After the crowd dispersed to resume their usual activities, their former comrades were left to experience the joys of prison life. I took the opportunity to inquire of Foster whether he trusted his hired hands. To my surprise, he responded with a twinkle in his eye, assuring me that Miller and Bass would have fled before the morning. And he was correct. The following day, as I approached the lower end of town, I witnessed the same group of onlookers, now augmented by more curious men and young boys, congregating to pay their respects to the new establishment. The jailer and guard were present, proclaiming and explaining their duties with great enthusiasm. However, like the rest of the hard-working citizens, they had dozed off, and during their slumber, the prisoners had managed to create a hole and escape. Foster examined the hole and then enlisted a young boy to attempt to crawl through it. The lad got stuck in the middle and had to be rescued with considerable effort. The crowd was delighted by this spectacle. Without hesitation, Foster pushed the jailer and guard into the jail, firmly shut, bolted, and chained the iron door, and pocketed the key. He then spent the entire day inside the jail, ignoring the threats of his prisoners. As the evening approached, and having gone without a drink for much longer than usual, the prisoners began to plead with Foster, but he was deaf to their entreaties. At dusk, he left the jail and instructed me to help him keep watch that night. We roamed around the outskirts of town, carrying two heavy double-barreled shotguns that Foster had secured from somewhere, and took up a position behind some bushes in the lot adjacent to the jail. We waited for something to happen. Foster was not above getting even with these fellows. Throughout the early part of the night, groups of six or more men came down the street and enjoyed their final treat at the expense of the jailer and guard.

The inmates were yelling for "drink" instead of water, and the more they shouted, the louder the laughter of those outside grew. The last group of people departed around ten o'clock, leaving the prisoners feeling hopeless and parched. My companion, Foster, and I had been thoroughly entertained by the spectacle and believed that the best part of the show was yet to come. The moon was visible, but its light was somewhat obscured by clouds, illuminating the night. We were positioned about 60 yards away from the prison and slightly above it, which gave us an excellent view of the entrance. At around eleven o'clock, we heard soft footsteps coming from behind the jail, followed by two shadowy figures who soon emerged in front of us. They placed something on the ground, which made a metallic sound like a crowbar. We could hear whispering, then low, coarse laughter. The rescuers, who we assumed were Miller and Bass, began to open the door. They started quietly at first, but the door was sturdy and they were not fond of exerting themselves. They began to swear and make noise. Foster whispered to me that we should wait until the door was opened and then fire both barrels when all four were in sight. We could have easily descended and apprehended the rescuers, but that was not Foster's intention. He preferred to use cunning against their craftiness; he believed it was the most effective way to gain their respect. The workers had to stop four times, and once they were so irritated with the prisoners' demands to delay the process to fetch a bottle that they threatened to abandon the project entirely. However, they were persuaded to stay and try again. Finally, the door gave way with enough noise to wake up people living a block away. The rescuers and rescued emerged from the jail, grunting with satisfaction and laughter.

In an instant, Foster and I pulled the triggers on both barrels, the sounds coming together in a thunderous boom. The group of men in front of us broke apart like scattered mercury. Two of them fell to the ground, while the others ran away, screaming in pain and fear. The ones who fell got up, limping and hobbling, before joining their comrades in a slow retreat. It was clear they would be feeling the pain for a long time.

The next morning, over breakfast, Dick regaled me with a story about how we had turned the tables on those jokers. It seemed like the whole town knew about it already, which was surprising. Even if Foster had killed those men, the townsfolk wouldn't have turned on us so quickly. The Ranger was not to be trifled with.

Later, I went for a ride with the girls, who were eager to know what had happened. I was suddenly a news-carrier, and Miss Barkley was more than curious. She found the story of our jailbreak amusing, and Gwen laughed heartily. Diane, on the other hand, had a different question. She wanted to know about a rumor she had heard about Reuben Darling, that he had shot himself with a gun and was unable to leave his house. When she asked her father about it, he became angry and refused to answer at first. When she persisted, he finally gave her a curt response: "Yes, the damn fool got himself shot, and I'm sorry it's not worse." Diane was puzzled by her father's reaction and asked me what I thought of it.

"Isn't he cheerful and kind?" Gwen said, laughing. I joined in, but I didn't want to talk about Reuben's accident. I couldn't stand the thought of Darling and the inevitable harm he would bring to his cousins. Gwen didn't make it easy for me to avoid her. She was sweet and charming, and I had been avoiding her since the dance. I didn't know if she was genuinely sorry for her outburst or if she was trying to ruin my peace. I made sure we were never alone because I didn't trust myself if she ever got too close. Despite all this, I enjoyed the ride with the girls. There was something special about being in their company. Plus, Miss Barkley's growing curiosity about Foster was entertaining. I pretended to be reluctant to talk about him, but I dropped subtle hints and stories that hinted at his bravery. I never mentioned the incident that shocked her before. I couldn't guess what was on her mind, but I knew she had a generous heart and wasn't satisfied with her father's opinion of the Ranger. She was like any other girl, admiring bravery and weaving romantic tales.

The town was still talking about the jail incident, and one detail that sparked curiosity was Storekeeper Roberts' role in informing on his attackers. Foster and I were waiting to see what would happen next. When would the town wake up to the importance of having a Ranger around?

Just three days later, Ranger Foster came to me with a story about a woman who had approached him on the street. She was a hardworking, honest woman whose husband enjoyed gambling a bit too much. Unfortunately, he had been cheated out of his money at Jack Martin's saloon. This was not an uncommon occurrence, as other wives had made similar complaints. Ranger Foster saw this as an opportunity to help the women of Linrock and asked the woman, whose name was Vallimont, how much her husband had lost. She told him the amount, and he promised that if he found evidence of cheating, he would not only get the money back but also shut down Martin's place.

Ranger Foster instructed me to go to the saloon that night and get in the game. I complied and pretended to be drunk to avoid being scrutinized by the dealer. By nine o'clock, I had studied the game well, and it was clear that it was a highly crooked one. Foster arrived, and we had agreed on a sign beforehand. He was not as skilled in gambling as I was, so I was to give him a signal if I saw any cheating. However, I was in no rush to do so, as I noticed a freckle-faced cattleman in the game who had already lost a significant amount of money. He had sold some cattle that day and was on his way to Del Rio with his earnings. I didn't want him to lose any more.

Foster stood behind us, and I could sense his presence. He had an effect on the others, particularly the dealer, who was honest while Foster was watching. But as soon as Foster shifted his attention to other tables, the dealer resumed his crooked ways. It was a blatant robbery, and I knew we had to act fast to help the poor, hardworking people of Linrock.

As I sat at the gambling table, I couldn't help but notice the little cattleman next to me. He seemed harmless enough, but then he suddenly leaned over with fire in his eyes and gun in hand. I was ready to cause a scene, but the cattleman proved to be a sharper and more daring gambler than I had thought.

It looked like there might be a shootout right then and there if Foster hadn't intervened. He yelled out and jumped towards our table, telling the cattleman to put his gun away. The cattleman didn't budge and demanded to know who Foster was.

"I'm Foster. Put up your gun," he replied calmly.

It turned out that Foster was a Ranger, and the cattleman begrudgingly put his gun away. However, he wasn't ready to let the matter go just yet. He claimed that he had been robbed and demanded his money back.

Everyone at the table sat quietly while the cattleman held his gun leveled. Foster wanted to confirm whether the game was crooked, so he questioned each player one by one. To my surprise, one of them admitted that the game wasn't straight.

When Foster asked me what I thought, I didn't hold back. "Worse'n a hold-up, Mr. Ranger," I said, eager to prove my point. With some deft moves, I showed everyone how the dealer was cheating.

The other players from different tables gathered around us, curious and muttering. Just then, Martin walked in. He didn't look too friendly.

"What's this holler?" he asked, eyeing everyone warily. When he saw the cattleman's gun still pointed at the dealer, he knew what was going on.

"Martin, you know what it's for. Take your dealer and leave unless you want to see me clean out your place," Foster warned.

Martin looked sullen and fierce, but he knew better than to mess with a Ranger. With a grunt, he took the dealer and left the place. The crowd dispersed, and Foster backed up against the wall, ready for anything.

The rancher stood up slowly, pulling out another gun, and he definitely looked serious to me. "Well, Ranger, I reckon I'll stick around and make sure you're not causing any trouble," he said. "Listen up, friend," he continued, gesturing toward me with one of his guns, "just hand over the money you owe. We'll settle up after this little show."

I reached out and collected the large sum of money in front of me, pocketing it as I stood up, prepared for whatever might happen next. "Everyone give me some space!" yelled Foster at Martin and his intimidated crew. Foster scanned the room, searching for some sort of tool. He spotted a heavy axe in the corner, grabbed it, and began swinging it around like a whip as he advanced toward the faro table. The crowd backed away, inching closer to the door. With one powerful blow, Foster destroyed the dealer's box and table, sending them crashing into the scattered chairs. Then the towering Ranger proceeded to wreak further havoc. Martin's establishment was rough and basic, like a thousand other similar places - a large room with adobe walls, a rudimentary bar made of boards, piles of kegs in one corner, a stove, and a few tables with chairs. Foster only needed one blow to destroy each item he struck. He smashed in the top of every keg, causing the dark liquid to spill out. Martin cursed, and the crowd followed suit. That was a significant loss!

The small rancher, holding the men at gunpoint, backed them out of the room. Martin needed a stern warning to leave entirely. I followed them out, not wanting to miss any of the gang's actions. Right behind me came the cool, daring Texan who I admired. He had Martin figured out perfectly, as there was no sign of any resistance.

Amidst the shouts and cheers of the crowd, Foster's ax struck the walls of Martin's saloon. The sound of sodden thuds and red dust pouring out of the door signaled that Foster was making headway. The old adobe bricks crumbled easily under his skilled hands. First, the back wall fell, and then half of the front of the building. Foster emerged from the dust, wet with sweat, dirt covering his body, and his hair disheveled. He was a man of great stature and muscular development, exuding physical strength and energy. His somber face, with big gray eyes like open furnaces, expressed a passion equal to his strength. Only then did the wild and lawless town of Linrock truly understand the significance of this Ranger.

Foster threw the ax at Martin's feet. "Martin, don't you dare reopen here," he said curtly. "Don't start another place in Linrock. If you do, you'll be in jail at Austin for years." Martin, livid and scowling, slunk away with his cronies. Foster then returned the money that had been taken and divided the remaining sum with the other players. He walked away through the crowd, confident that no one would dare to attack him from behind.

The little cattleman exclaimed, "Well, damn me! So that's Texas Ranger Foster, hey? Never seen him before. All Texas, that Ranger!" I stayed downtown, enjoying the sensation and hearing different points of view. In just one hour, every male resident of Linrock and almost every female had viewed the wreckage of Martin's place.

The commotion was intense, as if a fire had erupted. People were speaking their minds without reservation, something they wouldn't have done in a more tranquil setting. The women, especially, were vocal, and I mentally recorded their comments. "Did he do it all alone?" "Thank goodness a man's come to Linrock!" "Well done, Molly Vallimont!" "This will bring tough times to Linrock." The women's satisfaction was a testament to the Ranger's approach to law enforcement. The men, however, including Blandy, owner of the Hope So, and his ilk, as well as the bunch of idle gamblers, storekeepers, ranchers, and cowboys, were all dubious or sullen. The absence of humor was striking. Foster had exposed his hand, and as one gambler remarked, "It's a difficult hand to play." In reality, the Ranger Service was loathed by the easygoing Texans who preferred anything but hard, honest labor, and it was detested by the lawless. Foster's authority was now evident to all, and it had no limits; it could extend as far as he could take it. Given the current state of affairs, his power could be substantial. The efforts of native sheriffs and constables in western Texas had been a joke, an utter flop. If an upstanding member of a community decided to become a sheriff, he immediately became a target for rowdy cowboys and other vicious groups. Many towns south and west of San Antonio owed their tranquility and prosperity to the Rangers and only to them. They had killed or expelled the criminals. They interpreted the law for themselves, and only such an uncompromising, unrelenting, and inexorable approach to law enforcement that resulted in the extermination of the lawless would achieve for all of Texas what it had done for some parts.

Foster was the catalyst that sparked a division within Linrock, separating the honest from the dominant dishonest. It was clear that Foster's life was in danger, as one disgruntled man growled, "What the hell are we up against? Ain't somebody gonna plug this Ranger?" However, what Foster represented was much more than just his own life - he stood for the Ranger Service, a force that helped, saved, defended, and punished with a somber menace of death that seemed to be embodied in his cold attitude toward resistance. This idea took hold of both the black and honest hearts of Linrock, making Foster more than just an officer, but a man who loomed up as the embodiment of a powerful force.

As I arrived at the ranch, Miss Barkley and Gwen eagerly recounted their encounter with Foster on the main street, describing him as grand. I proceeded to tell them the whole story in detail, confirming that everything was true. Diane asked me earnestly, "Tim, is it true, just as you tell it?" I assured her that it was, recounting how Mrs. Vallimont had gone to Foster with her troubles, how I had been in Martin's place when Foster entered, and how I had seen him wreck Martin's place and forbid him from starting another in Linrock.

Diane acknowledged Foster's actions, whispering softly to herself, "Then he does do splendid things." It was clear that Foster's reputation as a Ranger, long known to the lawless Pecos gang but previously considered a vague and distant thing, had become an actuality in Linrock. He was a Ranger in the flesh, whose surprising attributes included both the law and the enforcement of it.

I continued walking, catching a glimpse of Colonel Barkley in the background. Before I reached the corrals, Gwen came running after me, looking flushed and excited. "Tim, my uncle wants to see you," she said. "He's in a bad mood. Please don't lose yours." She even took my hand. Gwen was like a child in every way except for her fatal habit of flirting. Her sudden statement shook me out of any further thoughts about her. Why did Barkley want to see me? He never paid me any attention. I dreaded facing him, not out of fear but because I knew I would see more and more signs of guilt in Diane's father.

He was waiting for me on the porch, dressed in his usual riding attire. However, it seemed like he hadn't been out so far that day. He looked worn out and there was a furtive shadow in his eyes. Despite Gwen's conviction, his haughty and imperious temperament seemed to be in abeyance. "Tim, what have you heard about Martin's saloon being cleaned out?" he asked. "Dick can't give me any details."

I told the colonel what had happened, briefly and concisely. He chewed on his cigar before spitting it out with an unintelligible exclamation. "Martin's no worse than others," he said. "Blandy leans towards crooked faro. I've tried to stop that, anyway. If Foster can, more power to him!"

Barkley turned around and left me with a strange feeling of surprise and pity. He had surprised me before, but I had never felt any sympathy for him. It was possible that Barkley was indeed powerless, regardless of his position. I had known men before who had become involved in crime, yet were too manly to sanction a crookedness they could not help. Miss Barkley was standing in her doorway. I could tell she had heard everything and she looked agitated. I knew she had been talking to her father. "Tim, he hates the Ranger," she said. "That's what I'm afraid of. It'll bring trouble on us. Besides, like everybody here, he's biased."

He ain't got no love for Foster, but he still says "More power to him!" I don't get it, and I'm stuck in the middle!Foster's latest accomplishment was something new to me and strange to Linrock. I heard a lot about it from my friends, a little from Foster himself, and I witnessed the final incident firsthand. Andy Vey was an old rustler who had fallen on hard times and spent his days hanging around places where younger, better men like him gathered. Since he was a parasite, he was often kicked out of these places. On top of that, it was common knowledge that he had rustled in the past, and most of Linrock's citizens didn't know that the men he associated with were also rustlers. One night, Vey was badly beaten in a back room of a saloon and thrown out into an empty lot, where he lay all night and the next day. He probably would have died if Foster hadn't come along. The Ranger found the battered rustler, took him home, tended to his wounds, nursed him back to health, and spent several days with him in his little adobe house. During this time, I saw Foster twice at our meeting spot at night. He didn't have much to say, but he was eager to hear about Jim Dempsey, Morton, Darling, Barkley, and any other news I had about them and what was happening in town. Andy Vey eventually recovered, and I was lucky enough to be at the Hope So when he showed up and addressed a group of gamblers. "Folks," he said, "I'm saying goodbye to those who used to be my friends. I'm leaving Linrock. And I'm asking some of you to pass on my farewell and a goodbye message to those who did me wrong. I'm not saying that if I had met this Ranger years ago, I would have turned my life around and gone straight. But I'm leaving, and that's that."

Maybe I would, maybe. There's a lot a man doesn't know until it's too late. I'm old now, ready for the bone pile, and it doesn't matter. But I still have a sharp mind, and I want to give a tip to the gang who wronged me. And that tip needs to make its way up to the big guns of Pecos.

"This Texas Star Ranger was the man who took me in. I would have died like a poisoned coyote without him. And he talked to me. He even gave me money to leave Pecos. Maybe everyone will think he helped me because he wanted me to snitch. To tell them who's who around these rustler hangouts. Well, he never asked me. Maybe he saw that I wasn't a snitch. But I don't think he would ask anyone that, no matter what.

"And here's my tip. Foster has his sights set on the group. That might not mean much, but I've been around him, and I know how to read men. Just as sure as God made little apples, he's either going to take them down or he's going to kill them!"

Chapter Six.

It was odd that recounting this story had a negative effect on Diane Barkley. When I shared it with her, she initially displayed a glimmer of happiness, as any woman might at the mention of a noble deed. But then she grew pensive, almost gloomy and sad. I couldn't quite grasp the complexity of her emotions. Maybe she was comparing Foster to her father or perhaps she was desperate to believe in Foster but couldn't. It's possible that she suddenly saw the Ranger for who he truly was, to her detriment. She instructed me to take Gwen out for a ride and retreated to her room. I had a feeling Gwen had something up her sleeve when she emerged in her cowgirl outfit, eyeing me as if she was ready for battle. But she rode ahead of me for a long while before she put any of her schemes into action.

The first person I encountered had an air of respect, but there was something brewing inside her. "Hey Tim, can you tighten my cinch?" she asked as I caught up with her. I dismounted my horse and adjusted her cinch by pulling it up a notch and securing it. "My boot's unlaced too," she added, slipping her foot out of the stirrup. Her boot was very much unlaced, so I took off my gloves to lace it up. I did it with a calm demeanor, but deep down, I wanted to grab her and hold her tight or do something foolish. "Tim, I think Diane's in love with Foster," she said seriously, with the trust she sometimes showed me. "It's not surprising. It's in the air," I replied. She looked at me skeptically. "It was," she responded coyly. "The fickleness of women is not new to me. I didn't expect Waters to last long." "Certainly not when there are nicer guys around. One, in particular, when he cares," she said. Her little brown hand slipped out of her glove and landed on my shoulder. "Let's make up. You've been mean lately. Let's make up," she said. It wasn't what she said, but the pleasant tone of her voice and her proximity that made my heart race. My face grew hot, and I felt the blood rush to my cheeks. "Why should I make up with you?" I asked, trying to defend myself. "You're just flirting. You won't and can't be anything to me, really." Gwen leaned over me, and I couldn't look up. "Let's forget about reality," she said. "The future is far away. We're together now. I like you, Tim. And I need to be loved. I've never confessed that to any other man. You've been awful when we could have had so much fun. Riding in the sun, in the open, with the wind in our faces."

Walking in the moonlight at night was a romantic notion, but Tim had missed something important. He couldn't resist the sweetness and seductiveness of the girl he was with, but her naturalness and truth were just as irresistible. He trembled as he looked up at her flushed face and arch eyes. He knew he had to frighten her out of this daring mood or he would have to yield, even though he believed she was only trifling with him. As a man, he had to be unyielding, but he felt a surge of emotion that made him shake. He grasped her tightly, hurting her, and spoke hard, passionate truth.

"Girl, you're playing with fire!" he cried out hoarsely. "I love you, love you as I'd want my sister loved. I asked you to marry me. That was proof, if it was foolish. Even if you were on the level, which you're not, we could never be anything to each other. Understand? There's a reason, besides you being above me. I can't stand it. Stop playing with me or I'll..."

He didn't finish his sentence because Gwen turned deathly white. He let go of her and stepped back, trying to choke down his emotions.

"Tim!" she faltered. Her voice trembled with fear, but also with womanliness and regret. "I...I am on the level."

That statement touched the real heart of the girl.

"I'll play fair, Tim," I responded sternly. "I won't tease or coax you again. And if I do, I'll deserve whatever punishment I get. But don't think I'm a liar." We rode home in silence, Gwen's horse loping ahead of mine. As we approached the ranch, she slowed down so we could ride side by side. At the corrals, she asked me if I agreed with her about Diane. "Maybe you're right," I admitted. "I hope she's fallen for Foster." I regretted my words as soon as they left my mouth, knowing I couldn't outsmart women like I could men. Gwen didn't respond, simply saying goodnight before leaving.

That night, I told Foster about how Miss Barkley reacted to his kindness towards Vey. He couldn't hide his emotions, and I could tell he was eager for more information. I described how Diane looked, how her expressions changed with her emotions, and how she sounded when admitting her father's hatred towards Foster. I knew she was caught between two sides, and Foster's eyes showed he was hungry for any insight into her feelings.

I could tell he was anxious to hear any news about her, so I did my best to satisfy his curiosity. After exhausting all my information and imagination, he accused me of being an old woman for gossip. I was taken aback by his statement and could only stare at him. His curiosity had turned into irritation and then sadness as he spoke to me.

He apologized for his behavior and explained that even though they were Rangers, they were still human. He revealed that two sweet and lovable girls, including Miss Barkley, had crossed their dangerous path. He hoped that by doing their duty as Rangers, they could somehow do right by these innocent girls. He asked me, as his friend, to not speak of Miss Barkley again.

As I walked away, the shadows and stars above me, I felt sober and sick at heart for Foster and for myself. I wondered what the end of this fateful adventure would be. I also noticed a change in Miss Barkley. She became restless and wanted to ride and see for herself what was happening in Linrock. She demanded much of my time, leaving me with little time to be near Foster until after dark.

As the rustlers played their waiting game, Dempsey slowly gathered trustworthy men to form a band until they were ready to strike. Foster knew it was best to go slow until the organization was complete. I could not help but worry about the situation, but there was little use in remonstrating with Miss Barkley. She refused to obey her father, who desperately pleaded with her to go back to

Louisiana for her own safety. Barkley loved his daughter, despite being an unscrupulous man. He suggested they sell their property, take their best horses and go back to their old home to live out their lives, but she refused to leave Linrock.

Miss Barkley was drawn to the free, unfettered life of the country and the thrill of riding. Even though her father forbade her from leaving the ranch, she refused to obey. When Barkley came to me, he confided that he had wanted to get rid of me before but had changed his mind. Diane, his daughter, had always been a spoiled kid, but now she was a woman with something firing her blood. Perhaps it was the wild country that had gotten to her, but she had the bit between her teeth and would run until she was exhausted.

Now, the safety of Diane and Gwen, too, had fallen into my hands as the girls refused to have any of Barkley's cowboys near them. It was a challenging situation, but I knew I had to do my best to protect them.

Recently, folks around here have been avoiding Reuben. I'll tell you, conditions in Pecos have been worse than they've appeared since y'all arrived at the ranch. It won't be long before trouble breaks out again. "I can't stop it. The toughest gang in western Texas will fill the town. My daughter and Gwen wouldn't be safe if they were left alone to go anywhere. But with you, maybe they'll be safe. Can I count on you?"

"Absolutely, Barkley," I replied. "I'm on good terms with most folks in town. I think it's safe to say that none of the tough guys who hang out down there would make a move while I'm with the girls. But I'll be careful to avoid them, especially any strangers who might show up. And if they do start trouble, I'll pull out my gun. There won't be any talking."

"Good! I've got your back," Barkley said. "Listen, Tim, I didn't want you here, but I always knew you were tough, a man not to be messed with. You've got a bad reputation. Diane thinks your reputation is undeserved. She'd trust you with herself no matter what. And Gwen, well, she'd like you if it weren't for the drinking. Have you been drunk a lot? Be honest with me."

"Not even once," I replied. "Reuben must be lying. He's had it out for me ever since that day in Sanderson. Watch out for him, though. He's got a temper, and when he's drinking, he's a real devil. I've taken a lot from Darling, and I guess I can take more."

"Okay, Tim," Barkley said, sounding relieved. "Put away the booze and cards for a while and keep an eye on the girls. When my business is sorted out, maybe I'll have an offer for you."

Barkley's words gave me a lot to think about.

Maybe it wasn't just the fact that a Ranger was in town that was bothering Barkley. It could have been the internal conflict within the rustler gang that he was associated with. The threat of being exposed to the public could be the reason for his agitation. As I got to know Barkley better, I couldn't find any evidence of his personal wrongdoing, and I felt sorry for him. At first, he didn't like me because I wasn't the cowboy he wanted, but our recent conversation proved that he had no idea I wasn't one of them. I also noticed that he seemed to be losing his patience with Darling, and there was a hint of fear and distrust in his tone when he talked about him. It's possible that the clash between Barkley and Darling was over Diane, but I thought it was absurd.

As I left the rowdy life in the saloons and gambling halls behind and spent my days under the blue sky and stars, my soul was lifted. I was happy to be done with that job. It was bad enough to have to go into those dens to arrest men, let alone live with them and almost become one of them. Diane noticed a change in me and attributed it to the fact that I wasn't drinking anymore, and she was pleased. Gwen was overjoyed, and to my dismay, she broke her promise not to tempt or tease me anymore. She was irresistible, and we rode every day and almost all day long.

After finishing our dinner, we headed towards the foothills, riding until the sun began to set. Our journey took us to remote ranches, water-holes, and old adobe houses that had once been the site of battles between rustlers and ranchers. We even rode to the small village of Barkley, halfway to Sanderson, and all over the countryside. But Miss Barkley was not content with just any ride; she craved new places, faces, and adventures. Every time we went out, she insisted on riding through Linrock, and every time we returned, she demanded we go back that way. We visited every store, blacksmith, wagon shop, and feed and grain house she could find an excuse to visit. I had to point out all the disreputable establishments in town and all the unsavory characters we encountered. She even wanted to see the inside of the infamous Hope So, much to the establishment's confusion. I pretended not to notice her restless curiosity, but Gwen understood, and it divided her between a sweet gravity and a mischievous humor. However, she never displayed the latter in front of Diane.

It seemed that we were destined to cross paths with Vaughn Foster. We spotted him working around his adobe house, then on horseback. Once, we even came face to face with him in a store. He stared straight into Diane Barkley's eyes and continued on his way without acknowledging her. Her face turned red as he passed, then white once he was gone. That day, she rode recklessly, almost putting her life in danger, completely oblivious to her horse's well-being. Another day, we found Foster in the valley, where we discovered he had gone to the home of an ill, elderly cattleman who lived alone.

The final meeting that proved most significant was when we were walking our tired horses through the main street of Linrock. We stumbled upon Foster just in time to witness him in action. We were passing a corner where a group of usual slack-jawed, shirtless loafers were gathered. They were having a grand old time at the expense of a poor ruffian who had either purchased or been given a frail, emaciated little burro that was on its last legs. Clearly, the burro did not want to go with its new owner who yanked on the halter, viciously swinging the end of the rope to leave welts on the worn and scarred back of the animal. Diane Barkley, who had a deep love for horses and detested the sight of spurs or whips, could not bear to see an animal in pain. When she saw the man beating the little burro, she cried out to me, "Make that brute stop!"

I would have made a move to intervene, but at that moment, I saw Foster emerging from around the corner. Just then, the despicable character named Andrews, whom I recognized as the man beating the burro, began to unleash heavy and brutal kicks upon the animal's body. The sound of the kicks was deep, hollow, and almost like a drumbeat. The burro let out a strange sound that I had never heard come from any other creature, and it collapsed with jerking legs that any horseman would recognize as a sign of grave injury. Foster saw the last swings of Andrews's heavy boot and let out a sharp yell that would have startled anyone. Unfortunately, it was too late, and the burro had already fallen.

Foster knocked over several of the jeering men to get to Andrews, kicking the fellow's feet from under him, sending him crashing to the ground. Then, Foster picked up the end of the halter and began to swing it powerfully, delivering resounding smacks that were mixed with hoarse bellows of fury and pain.

Andrews struggled to stand up, but the heavy knotted halter kept knocking him down. Foster eventually stopped, and Andrews stood up in front of him. He was acting like a madman and went for his gun, but Foster was quick to intercept it. Foster grabbed Andrews' arm, and there was a loud crack as bones broke and Andrews screamed in agony. The gun fell into the dirt, and in a fit of rage, Andrews lay beside it, broken and beaten. Foster stood there calmly, daring anyone to make a move, but no one did. He eventually walked away, leaving us all in shock.

Miss Barkley didn't say anything the rest of the ride home, but she looked pale and troubled. Gwen couldn't stop talking about what had just happened, and I couldn't help but feel that Diane Barkley was destined to fall in love with Vaughn Foster. I couldn't read her mind, but I knew what I felt.

The next day, as we were riding home, I saw a group of dark horses and riders quickly approaching us. We were on the main road, in plain sight of the town and passing by ranches, but I couldn't shake off the feeling that something was off.

I didn't think it was necessary to race our horses just to get to town a little earlier than these strangers. As a result, they caught up with us quickly. There were five of them, all with dark faces except for one, who was dressed in dark clothing and mounted on a dark bay or black horse. They had no pack animals and didn't seem to be carrying any packs. Four of them passed us at a gallop, while the fifth matched our pace and rode between Gwen and me.

"Good day," he said to me in a friendly tone. "I hope you don't mind if I ride with you all?"

Given his pleasant demeanor, I couldn't help but be polite. He was a remarkably handsome man, under forty years old, with curly blond hair that was almost golden, a fair complexion for that region, and the clearest, boldest blue eyes I had ever seen in a man.

"You must be Tim," he said. "Some of my men have seen you riding around with Barkley's girls. I'm Jack Blome."

He didn't say his name with any arrogance or pomp. He simply stated it. Blome, the rustler! I felt uneasy all over. Nevertheless, it appeared that there was nothing for me to do but return his kindness. I felt less nervous after he introduced himself. I introduced him to the girls without any awkwardness. He took off his hat and made a gallant bow to both of them. Miss Barkley had heard of him and his reputation, and she couldn't help but become pale and shrink back, although he didn't seem to notice. Gwen had been eager to meet a real rustler, and here he was, the prince of rascals. However, I sensed that she would need some time before she felt comfortable. Blome appeared to be more interested in Gwen than in Diane.

"Do you like Pecos?" he asked Gwen.

"Out here? Oh, yes, indeed!" she responded.

"Do you like to ride?" he asked.

"I love horses," Gwen replied. Like most men who met Gwen, he quickly realized that talking about horses was the best way to keep her interested. He clearly loved thoroughbred horses himself, and spoke to Gwen with genuine interest. He could have been anyone, but there was something different about him. He was a desperado, one of the reckless and daring kind that were known along the Pecos and Rio Grande. He wore clothes that were not typical of most Westerners, made of silk, velvet, and fine leather. His spurs were worth coveting, and he carried a short rifle and a gun in saddle-sheaths. As I looked him over, I noticed a row of notches on the bone handle of his Colt, indicating the number of men he had killed. This made my blood boil, as I was a Ranger and such practices were abhorrent to me.

As we reached the edge of town, Blome doffed his hat and rode off ahead of us. I found it difficult to keep up with the excited chatter of the two young ladies. Miss Langdon was particularly taken with Blome, saying that she could adore him. Miss Barkley also joined in with compliments for the rustler. I needed time to think, but their chatter made it difficult.

My frustration was a sign that my thoughts were turning to anger. "Jack Blome!" I interrupted their praises. "He's a rustler and a gunman. Did you notice the marks on his gun? Each mark represents a man he's killed! For weeks, we've been hearing rumors in Linrock that he's planning to come here and get rid of that troublesome Texas Ranger, Vaughn Foster!"

Chapter Seven.

The weight of my words hit me hard as I watched Gwen's heart break before me. "Oh, Tim! No! No!" she cried out. Diane Barkley stood nearby, her eyes fixed on the hill and the ranch in front of us. Though her gaze was distant, I could see the truth in her eyes - she loved Foster.

I couldn't bear to leave Miss Barkley with the impression that I had intended. My own emotions were twisted, as I had once suffered through love and now I reveled in seeing her suffer the same fate. But now that my cruel desire for her to love Foster had come true, I felt only pity for her and the enormity of my actions. It was a crime to make this noble and beautiful woman love a Ranger, the enemy of her father and the author of her future misery. I was horrified at what I had done.

Desperately, I tried to justify my actions with my old motive - that through her love we might all be saved. But it was too late, and I knew that my motive had been wrong and unjustified. We rode home in silence, Miss Barkley dismounting at a path leading to the trees and flowers. "I want to rest, to think before I go in," she said.

Gwen and I rode our horses to the corrals. As we approached the gate, I noticed the tears in her eyes and knew my fears had been confirmed. "Tim," she said, "it's worse than we thought."

"Worse? No kidding," I replied. "It's going to devastate her. She's never cared that much for anyone before. When the Barkley women love, they love hard."

"Well, at least you're a Langdon," Gwen retorted bitterly. "I'm Barkley enough to be miserable, but Langdon enough to have some sense. You, on the other hand, have no sense or kindness. Why did you have to blurt out that Jack Blome was here to kill Foster?"

"I'm ashamed, Gwen," I admitted, hanging my head. "I've been a brute. I wanted her to love Foster, for some stupid reason. I just wanted to see how much she cared. The other day you said misery loves company, and that's exactly what I've been doing. I've been bitter and angry, taking my frustration out on Miss Barkley. It was a damn unmanly thing for me to do."

"It's not that bad," Gwen replied gently. "But you could have been more tactful. Tim, you're taking a very tragic view of your own situation."

"Tragic? Ha!" I exclaimed, feeling like a villain in a play. "What other way is there to look at it? I love you so much it's consuming me."

"That's not tragic," Gwen said softly. "When you have no chance, that's tragic."

Gwen could shift moods quickly, and now she seemed warm, vulnerable, and sincere. I felt myself slipping, but managed to catch myself before saying anything foolish.

The bitter realization of renunciation made it easy for me to feign anger. "You promised not to do it again," I began, choking on my own words. My voice was hoarse and it broke, but I knew I couldn't pretend any longer. I had seen Gwen Langdon in various states of emotion before, but never like this. She was pale and trembling slightly. If it wasn't fear, then I couldn't tell what it was. But there was also a sense of contrition and earnestness about her.

"Tim, I know. I promised not to tease or tempt you anymore," she faltered. "I've broken it. I'm ashamed. I haven't played fair. But I can't help myself. I have enough sense not to engage myself to you, but I can't stop loving you. I can't leave you alone. There, I said it. What's more, I'll continue as I have unless you stay away from me. I don't care what I deserve or what you do. I will, I will!" She began faltering, but ended with a passionate outburst.

Somehow, I managed to keep my composure, even though my heart was pounding like a hammer and my blood was rushing in my ears. The thought of Foster saved me. But I felt a chill run down my spine at the narrow margin. I feared that a kiss or a single touch from this bewitching creature of fire and change and sweetness would make me put her before Foster and my duty.

"Gwen, if you dare break your promise again, you'll regret ever being born," I said with all the fierceness I could muster. "I already regret it. And you can't bluff me, Mr. Gambler. I may not have a hand to play, but you can't make me fold," she replied.

Something told me that Gwen Langdon was discovering herself, and that soon I wouldn't be able to scare her anymore. And then, I knew, I would be doomed.

"I don't want to distress you, Miss Barkley," I began, "but I must tell you something. Blome has come to Linrock after Foster. He intends to kill him."

Miss Barkley's face went white as a sheet. "Oh no," she whispered, "what can we do?"

"Well, I don't believe he can do it," I said confidently. "Blome's not man enough. But I wanted to let you know so you can be careful."

"Thank you, Mr. Adams," she said gratefully. "I will be careful."

As I walked away, I couldn't help but feel a sense of satisfaction. I had done the right thing by telling her, and I had also managed to keep my own feelings for Gwen hidden. It was a tricky situation, but I had handled it with all the coolness and strength of a seasoned cowboy.

The storm had passed and her pale face and calm demeanor showed it. Despite the situation at hand, she always had a smile for me. However, I felt guilty for betraying her trust. "Miss Barkley," I started, stumbling over my words. "I was thinking, maybe you're upset about this gunfighter, Blome, coming to kill Foster. At first, I thought it was because of the potential bloodshed, but then I realized you were interested in Foster's Ranger work. Maybe you care about him."

"Don't beat around the bush, Tim," she interrupted. "You know I care." Her eyes were a wonder to behold, dark and sad, with the soul of a woman at the bottom. I admired her honesty and was inspired to be truthful myself. "Listen," I said, "Blome has come to meet Foster, and there will be a fight. But Blome won't be able to kill Foster."

Miss Barkley was confused. "How is that possible? You said Blome was a killer with notches on his gun. Why won't he succeed?"

"Because Foster will be on the lookout, and Blome won't be quick enough on the draw to kill him. Foster is one of the best shots on the frontier, and I doubt there's anyone who could beat him in a fair fight."

Miss Barkley wanted to know more. "I understand, but tell me more about this fair fight. What do you mean?"

"Well, Blome is conceited, and he'll want to make the meeting fair. But even then, I don't think he'll be quick enough to beat Foster. It'll be a close one, but I believe Foster will come out on top."

Blome plans to search for Foster by making a big show of his presence. However, Foster is likely to avoid him for as long as he can. If they do come face to face, Blome will have to make the first move. Foster has a strange effect on people, and it will be interesting to see how Blome handles him. Blome may know of Foster's reputation, but he has never seen him in action. Foster is a master of handling a gun, and no one can beat him in a quick draw. There was an outlaw named Duane who might have been able to take down Foster, but he never got the chance. A girl saved Duane and turned him into a Ranger, and he left Texas for good.

The woman listening to this story finds it fascinating and wants to know more. She asks if it really comes down to the quickness of the hand when men face each other in this part of Texas. I confirm that it is all about the draw, and Foster is the best at it. I demonstrate my own quick draw, and the woman is impressed. She admits that it's horrible to be interested in such a thing, but she is caught up in the wildness of the frontier and is glad to know that Foster has the skill to protect himself.

"Thanks, Tim," she said as she stood up and turned away slightly. Then, she paused. One hand was on her chest and the other was on the bench. "Have you talked to him recently?" she asked, and a faint blush appeared on her cheeks. Her eyes were steady and deep, staring through me. "Yeah, I've run into him a few times around town," I replied.

"Did he ever mention me?" she asked.

"Once or twice, and he couldn't help it," I said.

"What did he say?" she asked.

"The last time I saw him, he seemed eager to hear about you. He didn't ask, but he was practically begging. So, I told him everything I knew about you - how you dressed, how you looked, what you said, what you did. I hope you're not offended, Miss Barkley. I tend to talk too much sometimes."

She didn't hear my apology or my plea. There was a certain glow in her eyes. As I looked at her, my vision became blurry and hazy. "What did he say?" she whispered shyly, and I could hardly believe that the proud Miss Barkley was standing before me.

"Well, he flew into a rage and called me a..." I stopped myself. "He said that if I wanted to talk to him again, I shouldn't mention you. He was being unreasonable."

"Tim, do you think he still..." She wasn't facing me anymore. Her head was bent down, and both of her hands were on her chest. I saw her chest heave, and her cheeks were white as a flower. Her neck was red with mounting blood. I understood what was happening. I pitied her, hated myself, and was amazed by this thing called love. It had turned Diane Barkley into a different woman.

I could hardly believe it when Diane Barkley came to me, practically begging for reassurance of Foster's love. As someone who knew nothing about women, this seemed odd to me. But then a thought hit me like a ton of bricks - had Diane figured out her father's guilt? Was it for his sake more than her own that she hoped Foster loved her? It was a mystery, and it gave me a lot to think about. Only a strong motive or an all-consuming love could make someone like Diane Barkley, who was so full of pride, ask such a question.

No matter the reason, I was determined to assure her that what I knew to be true. I spoke to her with all the emotion I could muster, telling her that I could see how much Foster loved her, how deeply and passionately. I also warned her that his love for her would make his work in Linrock extremely difficult. But she seemed to understand, and there was a stillness about her that reminded me of Gwen when I proposed to her.

"Tim, please bring us together," Diane pleaded. "You're our friend." And then she was gone, leaving me feeling both honored and cursed to have been chosen by Foster as his partner in this dangerous game.

Later that evening, I found myself in the girls' sitting room, where they asked me about the gunfighters, outlaws, and other dangerous men of the frontier. Diane and Gwen had been completely ignorant of such characters before moving to Texas, but now they were both fascinated and repelled by them. It seemed that Diane might have placed the Rangers in the same category as these dangerous men, just like her father and Governor Smith.

Gwen believed she had fallen for a cowboy who had a reputation as bad as they come. She was convinced he was the real deal. As for me, I knew a thing or two about dangerous and wicked men. Being from Texas, I was well-versed in the subject. It was a challenge to differentiate between the good and bad fighters. But spotting a genuine outlaw from a phony was easy for someone like me.

So, I regaled the girls with stories of notorious outlaws like Buck Duane, who was both an outlaw and a Ranger. I also shared the tales of Murrell, Hardin, Sandobal, Cheseldine, Bland, Alloway, King Fisher, Thompson, and Sterrett. These men were all still alive and kicking, leaving a trail of bloodshed and crime in their wake.

But I saved the best story for last. Amos Clark was unlike any other outlaw I had ever known. He was a man of influence and wealth, respected by his peers. He was an upstanding citizen who fought against rustlers and outlaws. But, as it turned out, he was the leader of a gang of rustlers, highwaymen, and murderers.

Captain Neal and his Rangers uncovered Clark's true identity and brought him to justice. He was arrested and eventually hanged for his crimes. It just goes to show that sometimes, the most dangerous men are the ones who hide in plain sight.

The case was one that stood out, showcasing what was possible in the untamed country. Clark had a son who was honest and a wife he cherished deeply. Both were entirely unaware of the darker side of life. I recounted this story deliberately, albeit with some concern. I needed to see if Miss Barkley was suspicious of her father, and to look into her eyes was no easy feat. However, when I did, I was shocked, though not in the way I anticipated. She knew something, perhaps more than Foster or I, but if it was a crime, she concealed her true feelings remarkably well.

Jack Blome and his men had been in Linrock for several days, accompanied by old Snecker, his son Bo, and other rough-looking individuals, unfamiliar to me but not to Linrock. They created a charged, anticipatory atmosphere. The saloons did unprecedented business and never closed. Respectable townspeople were roused from their slumber by rowdy carousing in the streets at dawn. Foster remained largely under cover, not believing, nor did I, that Blome and his gang would target him the first time he walked down the street. Such occurrences were rare, and when they did happen, it was more coincidence than intention. Blome was preparing the stage for his little play. Meanwhile, Foster was not idle. He informed me he had met Jim Dempsey, Morton, and Zimmer, and that these men had approached others of a similar ilk. A secret club had formed, and all members were primed for action. Foster had also spent hours at night observing the house where Reuben Darling stayed when he wasn't at Barkley's.

Darling had almost recovered from his arm injury, but he remained indoors most of the time. At night, his house was visited by strange, swift, and stealthy men who were previously strangers and not his neighbors. Foster could not recognize any of these visitors, and he did not think it was time to confront them. Jim Dempsey had declared that something was amiss, something different from Blome's intention of meeting the Ranger. Dempsey was correct. Within twenty-four hours of his conversation with Foster, where he recommended quick action, he was found dead behind the little room of his restaurant, with a bullet hole in his chest. No one heard any shots, and it was a deliberate murder since a piece of paper with the words "All friends of Ranger Foster look for the same" was left behind the bar.

Later that day, I met Foster at Dempsey's and accompanied him when he viewed the body and the written message that indicated hostility towards him. We left together, and I hoped he would allow me to stay with him from that moment on. "Tim, it's all in the dark," he said. "I believe Darling is involved."

I agreed. "I recall his face at Dempsey's when you wounded him. Jim insisted that you were wrong not to kill him instead of wounding him. You were wrong."

"No, Tim, I never let my emotions get the best of me. We can't prove anything against Darling."

"Let's find him. I bet I can accuse him and make him reveal his hand. Come on!"

Foster found it challenging to resist me, but that was all the satisfaction I received for my anger and desire to avenge Jim Dempsey, which consumed me.

"Listen up, son. You're gonna find yourself in a whole heap of trouble soon enough," Foster warned me. "Just hold tight and keep your eyes on Barkley at night. See if anyone's coming to visit him. Spy on him. I'll keep an eye on Darling."

"Don't you think it'd be better if you stayed out of town, especially at night?" I asked.

"Sure thing. I've got some blankets out in the brush, and I go there every night and leave before daylight. But I keep a light on in the adobe house to make it look like I'm there."

"Good idea. I was worried about that. Now, what's gonna happen with Morton, Zimmer, and their crew after Jim Dempsey's murder?"

"They're all seeing red, Tim. They're out for blood. If we need backup, I just have to say the word."

"Have you seen Blome around?"

"Once. I was across the street when he came out of the Hope So with some of his gang. They watched me, but I just kept going."

"He's looking for trouble, Foster."

"Yeah, and he'd have found it by now if I knew his connection to Barkley and Darling."

"Do you think he's a dangerous man to meet?"

"Not really. He's a genuine bad man, but he's not much to be feared. If he'd just keep away from trouble, that'd be a different story. Blome will probably die thinking he's the toughest and quickest draw in the West."

That settled my worries. "For now, let's help out Jim Dempsey's family," Foster suggested. "His wife's not doing too well. She's got a lot of kids, and Jim was poor. She told me her neighbors would avoid her now, out of fear."

"It's tough, but we can give Jim a decent burial and help out his family," Foster had said to me. A few days later, I took Miss Barkley and Gwen to visit Jim Dempsey's wife and children. I knew Foster would be there, but I didn't tell Miss Barkley. We rode to Mrs. Dempsey's little adobe house, which Foster and I had moved her and the children into after Jim's funeral. The house was small but cozy, and the yard was green and shady. To my knowledge, no one besides Foster and me had visited Mrs. Dempsey, so Miss Barkley packed a big basket full of food for them. I carried it in front of me on the saddle as we rode.

We tied our horses to the fence and went to the back of the house. Several children were playing on the small porch with a stone floor. The door was open, and Mrs. Dempsey invited us in when I knocked. Foster wasn't there, but we went in with the girls. "Mrs. Dempsey, I brought Miss Barkley and her cousin to see you," I said cheerfully. The little room wasn't very bright, with only one window and the door. Mrs. Dempsey lay on a bed, hollow-cheeked and haggard. Once she had been a woman of some beauty, but the ravages of trouble and grief were evident in her worn face. Her husband's face had been hard and bitter, but hers wasn't. I wondered how she would feel about the daughter of Barkley, who had ruined her husband. "So you're Roger Barkley's girl?" Mrs. Dempsey asked, her bright black eyes fixed on her visitor. "Yes," Miss Barkley replied simply.

"My cousin, Gwen Langdon and I are here to help you in any way we can," said Diane Barkley, introducing herself to Mrs. Dempsey. There was a moment of silence before Mrs. Dempsey spoke. "You do look a bit like Barkley, but you're not like him at all. You must take after your mother. Miss Barkley, I don't know if I should accept anything from you. Your father ruined my husband," she said.

Diane replied, "Yes, I know. That's why I want to help you even more. Please don't refuse. It would mean so much to me." Mrs. Dempsey's resentment quickly dissipated in the warmth and kindness of Diane's manner. Diane's beauty was quickly surpassed by her generosity and nobility. She won over the children and the mother with her charm and opened a big basket of food for them.

Meanwhile, I went out on the porch to avoid getting too emotional. I was angry at Jim Dempsey's killer and wished I could have laid my eyes on him. However, Diane and Gwen were practical and focused on bringing cheerfulness, kindness, and help to the family.

"Mrs. Dempsey, who dressed this baby?" asked Diane, pointing to a dilapidated youngster on the floor. "Mr. Foster," replied Mrs. Dempsey, choking on her words. Diane was shocked. "He's taken care of us all since...since..." Mrs. Dempsey couldn't finish her sentence.

Diane's practicality and kindness were a breath of fresh air for the Dempsey family. She and Gwen were determined to do what they could to help the family during this difficult time.

Miss Barkley quickly responded, "So, you've had no other help besides his? No other women have offered their assistance? That's a shame! I'll send someone over, Mrs. Dempsey, and I'll come myself."

The older woman replied, "That would be very kind of you. You see, Jim didn't have many friends in town, and the ones he did have were afraid to help us. They were afraid they would end up like poor Jim."

Miss Barkley was outraged and exclaimed, "What kind of friends are those? Mrs. Dempsey, don't worry anymore. We'll take care of you. Gwen, can you help me with the baby's dress?"

It was clear that Miss Barkley was having trouble controlling her emotions. Gwen chimed in, "Why, the dress is on backwards. I don't think Mr. Foster has much experience dressing babies."

"Well, he did the best he could," Mrs. Dempsey defended. "I don't know what would have happened to us without him. He brought your cowboy, Tim, who's been very helpful too."

"Mr. Foster, then, is he more than just a Ranger?" Miss Barkley asked, her voice breaking a little.

"He's more than I can explain," Mrs. Dempsey replied. "He buried Jim, paid off our debts, brought us here, bought us food, cooked for us, and even dressed and washed the baby. He sat with me for the first two nights after Jim passed away when I thought I was going to die myself. He's kind, patient, and gentle. He's kept me going just by being here. Sometimes I wake up from a nap and see him there, and I know how untrue all those rumors about him are. He plays with the children like any good man would. When he holds the baby, I can't believe he's the same man they call a ruthless killer."

"He's good, but he's not happy. He has these sad eyes and looks off into the distance sometimes when the children are playing around him. They love him, and I think he must have loved a woman once. His life seems so sad."

I ain't nobody to tell me they see good in everything. One time, this fella said someone had to be a Ranger. I tell ya, thank goodness for Rangers like him! After that, there was silence in the small room, except for the baby's cooing. I didn't dare peek at Miss Barkley. I was expecting Foster to show up, and his footsteps didn't surprise me. He came around the corner like he always does, quick and alert, with his hand ready. If I was an enemy waiting with a gun, I'd have to be fast. Foster was always on the defense.

"Hey there, son! How's Mrs. Dempsey and the little one today?" he asked.

"Hey yourself! They're doing great! I brought the girls down," I replied.

Then, in the semi-darkness of the room, Diane Barkley and Foster faced each other. It was a moment! After seeing her face, I wouldn't have missed it for anything. I'd never forget it as long as I lived. She didn't say anything, but Gwen bowed and spoke to the Ranger. Foster didn't show any unusual emotion after the initial start. He greeted both girls pleasantly.

"Tim, that was kind of you," he said. "It was women who were needed here. I could only do so much. Mrs. Dempsey, you look better today. I'm glad. And here's the baby, all clean and white. Baby, I had a hard time figuring out how your clothes went on! Well, Mrs. Dempsey, didn't I tell you friends would come? The brighter side will come too."

"Yes, I have more faith than before," replied Mrs. Dempsey. "Roger Barkley's daughter has come to me. After Jim's death, I thought I'd fall apart. We have nothing. How could I take care of my little ones? But I'm gaining courage."

"Mrs. Dempsey, don't worry anymore," said Miss Barkley.

"I promise you'll be taken care of, don't worry," I assured Mrs. Dempsey. Foster's expression lit up with gratitude. "Miss Barkley, that's great!" he exclaimed. "That's exactly what I had hoped for." The color rose in her cheeks at his praise. "And thank you, Miss Langdon, for coming," Foster added. "I'm grateful to have you both as allies in this lonely task. For the sake of this good woman and her children, I'm more than glad. But please be careful. Don't leave without Tim. It's dangerous out there." Foster backed towards the door and I followed. "Wait, Mr. Foster!" Miss Barkley called out after him. He made a strange sound and then kicked me so hard I thought he broke my leg. But I didn't say anything, I just watched as Diane Barkley stepped out of the door. She was stunning in her white dress. She didn't even notice me. "I was wrong about you," she confessed to Foster. I could see the emotion building inside him, but he remained calm. "Miss Barkley, there's no need to apologize. I understand why you believed what you did. But please don't say you wronged me."

As a Ranger, I know that many stories are told about me, and some of them are true. My duty is not always easy, and sometimes it falls hard on those who are innocent. But I also know that duty is hard on me.

One day, a woman named Miss Barkley approached me. She admitted that she had wronged a man named Foster, both in thought and in word. She had ordered him out of her home, believing him to be someone he was not. But she had been deceived, and now she realized her mistake.

Miss Barkley asked for forgiveness, and offered her hand to Foster. He took it, and held onto it tightly. I could see the struggle in his eyes, torn between the woman's charm and the knowledge of what she had done to him.

Miss Barkley continued, speaking with passion and intensity. She praised Foster for his kindness to another woman who had been alone and helpless. But she also revealed that she, too, was unfortunate. I wondered what had led her to this moment, burning with fire and passion.

In the end, Miss Barkley's words and actions left a deep impression on me. She had shown courage and humility, and had made amends for her past mistakes. And though I knew that duty was hard on me as a Ranger, I also knew that it was moments like these that made it all worth it.

"I may soon need a friend," I thought to myself. The person I need most to lean on is the one who is duty-bound to ruin me - Vaughn Foster. But I had to ask him, "Will you be my friend?" I knew that Diane Barkley would never ask anyone to be false to their duty. We both had to be true to her.

I felt so alone, with no one but Gwen who loved me. I knew that I would need a friend soon. "Oh, I know what you'll find out sooner or later. I know now! I want to help you. Let us save a life, if not honor. Must I stand alone?" My voice trailed off as I swayed towards Foster. I expected him to embrace me, but instead, he whispered hoarsely, "Diane Barkley, I love you! I must be true to my duty. But if I can't be true to you, then by God, I want no more of life!" He kissed my hand and rushed away.

I stood there, watching him vanish into the distance. Then, I turned to the only other person there - the one who had been listening to our conversation. I reached out to them, as a sister might reach out to a brother.

Chapter Eight.

We rode home in silence as the sun set on the horizon. Miss Barkley dismounted at the porch, while Gwen and I continued on to the corrals. I felt a sense of unease wash over me, as if impending doom was on the horizon.

"Can you help me down?" Gwen asked, her voice low and trembling.

"Gwen, did you hear what Miss Barkley said to Foster?" I inquired.

"I caught bits and pieces. I heard Foster confess his love for her. What a mess this is," Gwen replied.

"It certainly is. Did you hear why she asked Foster to be her friend?"

"No, I didn't hear that. I only heard her confess to wronging him," Gwen responded.

I tried to tune out the conversation between Gwen and whoever she was talking about. "Tell me," she had said. But it wasn't her secret to share. "I wish I could do something to help them somehow," the other person had replied. "Yes, it's a terrible situation. I don't care so much about myself."

"Nor me," Gwen retorted. "You! Oh, you're just a shallow, spoiled child. You'd stop loving anything the moment you won it. And me, well, I'm no good, you say. But their love! My God, what a tragedy! You have no idea, Gwen. They've hardly spoken to each other, yet are ready to be overwhelmed."

I sat there, still and silent, wondering if I had offended Gwen. But at that moment, I didn't really care. Her flirtatious behavior towards me and my own problems seemed insignificant. I didn't even look at her, even though she was close enough for me to feel her restless foot touching me. The horses in the corrals were coming up to the bars, and the sky was turning dark, except for a bright golden glow behind the mountains in the west.

"So I say you're no good?" Gwen asked after a long pause. Her voice and the way her hand touched my shoulder should have been a warning, but I didn't pay attention. "Yes, you said that, didn't you?" I replied absentmindedly.

"I can change my mind, can't I?" Gwen said. "Maybe you're only wild and reckless when you drink. Mrs. Dempsey said such nice things about you. They made me feel so good."

I didn't know how to respond to that, so I didn't say anything. Gwen swung herself around in the saddle. "Help me down," she said. Normally, she was very proud of her ability to dismount on her own, and would be insulted by an offer of help. But I didn't care. My spirit was dead.

Her hands slipped up my arms as she dismounted from her horse, and her face came close to mine. "Tim!" she whispered. Her voice was filled with torment, wistfulness, uncertainty, and tenderness all at once. I tried to reach for her hands, but they slipped away. She caught me off guard, and I kissed her without passion, filled with regret and sadness. She let out a little cry that mixed exultation with remorse for her victory and her broken faith. As soon as I kissed her, she remembered her broken faith. She trembled against me, leaving unsaid something she had meant to say, and ran away. She was undoubtedly frightened, and I thought it was for the best. Her spurs clinked away into the darkness, and I laughed ruefully, hoping she would be satisfied.

I put the horses away and went in for supper. Afterward, I noisily bustled around my room before sneaking out for my usual evening spying. The night was dark, with no starlight, and the stiff wind rustled the leaves and tore through the vines on the old house. Even though I had seen and heard little during my constant vigilance, the task never became monotonous or made me careless. I had so much to think about that sometimes I sat in one place for hours without realizing it.

That night, I heard Darling's well-known footsteps right away. Barkley's door opened, and a broad bar of light flashed into the darkness. Darling crossed the threshold, the door closed, and all was dark again outside. Not a ray of light escaped from the window. It had been a considerable amount of time since Darling's last visit, and I had no doubt that his conversation with Barkley would be interesting to me.

I cautiously approached the door and strained my ears, but all I could make out was a low hum of voices. It was too risky to stay there, so I made my way around the corner of the house. I had discovered something earlier that I believed would be useful - the older side of the adobe house had a narrow passage between the old and new walls, which led from the outside to the patio. I had stumbled upon it by chance, as it was hidden by vines and bushes. I had planned to drill a small hole through the adobe bricks, but I later realized that the wall was already cracked. I could see into Barkley's room through the crack. This passage was my chance, and I decided to take it despite the great danger. I crawled on my hands and knees, silently making my way under the shrubs to the entrance of the passage. In the darkness, a faint glimmer of light indicated the location of the crack in the wall. I had to enter sideways, squeezing through the narrow space without making a sound. The passage gradually widened in that direction, leading me to believe that the best escape route would be towards the patio. It took me a while to reach my destination, but once I did, the crack was a foot above my head. If only I were taller like Foster! I had to find toe-holds in the crumbling walls, bracing myself with my knees on one side and my back against the other to hold myself up to the crack.

As I gazed around the room, I could sense the tension in the air. Barkley sat there, twirling his mustache, his face clouded with concern. Darling, on the other hand, appeared even darker and more sullen, but there was a fierce determination in his eyes.

"We're settling both deals tonight," Darling declared, his voice full of authority. "That's why I've asked Snecker and Blome to be here."

Barkley looked impatient. "But what if I don't want to talk here?" he asked, clearly agitated. "I never before made my house a place to-"

"We've waited long enough," Darling interrupted, his tone firm. "This place is as good as any. You've lost your nerve since that Ranger hit town. First things first, will you give Diane to me?"

"You talk like a spoiled boy, Reuben," Barkley retorted. "Give Diane to you? She's a woman and I'm finding out that she's got a mind of her own. I told you I was willing for her to marry you. I tried to persuade her. But Diane hasn't any use for you now. She liked you at first, but now she doesn't. So what can I do?"

"You can make her marry me," Darling insisted.

Barkley shook his head. "Make that girl do what she doesn't want to? It couldn't be done, even if I tried. And I don't believe I'll try. I haven't the highest opinion of you as a prospective son-in-law, Reuben. But if Diane loved you, I would consent. We'd all go away together before this damned miserable business is out. Then she'd never know. And maybe you might be more like you used to be before the West ruined you. But as matters stand, you fight your own game with her, and I'll tell you now, you'll lose."

Darling grew increasingly agitated. "What did you want to let her come out here for?" he demanded. "It was a dead mistake. I've lost my head over her. I'll have her or die. Don't you think if she was my wife, I'd soon pull myself together? Since she came, we've none of us been right. And the gang has put up a holler."

"We have to settle this tonight, Barkley," I said firmly.

"Well, we can settle Diane's part right now," replied Barkley, getting up. "Come on, let's go ask her and see where you stand."

They left the door open as they went out. I sat down to rest and wait, wondering what Miss Barkley's response would be. But I had a feeling I already knew. Darling had proved to be just as bad as I had suspected, and I wished Foster was here to help me. However, he was too big to fit into this situation.

The men were gone for what seemed like a long time, but it was probably just my own interest and anxiety. Finally, I heard heavy footsteps. Darling came back in alone, looking defeated. However, his mood soon shifted to anger and he began to curse and pace the room.

Barkley returned, looking calmer. I could see that he was relieved at the rejection of Darling's proposal.

"Don't get mad, Reuben," he said. "I can't just give you my daughter like she's some unruly steer. We may be wild out here, but I have my limits."

"Barkley, I can make her marry me," declared Darling in a thick voice.

"How?" asked Barkley grimly.

"You know the hold I have on you from the deal that made you boss of this rustler gang," replied Darling. "I can go to Diane and tell her that I'll tell everyone, including Ranger Foster, unless she marries me."

Darling spoke breathlessly, with a haggard face and shadowed eyes. He had no shame, only a fierce passion. Barkley looked at him with a controlled fury, revealing a strong and unscrupulous man who had fallen into evil ways but was still a man. In contrast, Darling appeared to be a wild and passionate weakling.

As I observed the two men, it was clear that there had been a time when Barkley had supported Reuben Darling, despite the latter's weakness. However, that time had long passed, and Darling had become a self-centered and corrupt individual, like many others on the border. Barkley expressed concern that his daughter, Diane, should never find out about his involvement in rustling and thievery, but Darling was convinced that she already knew or would soon find out. He warned Barkley about Tim, Diane's cowboy companion, and his intelligence. Barkley tried to reassure Darling that Diane was preoccupied with his duties as mayor and certain property matters, but Darling was fixated on winning Diane's affections. He appeared desperate and determined to achieve his goal, even if it meant everyone going to hell. Barkley sat silently, stroking his mustache, his thoughts unclear.

With years of experience reading men in high-stress situations, I couldn't help but feel that Barkley had made up his mind to kill Darling. It was surprising to me that he hadn't reached this conclusion earlier. Perhaps the arrival of his daughter had put him at odds with himself. Suddenly, Barkley's dark expression disappeared, and he began to speak with urgency. Though his words were persuasive, I suspected he was only trying to calm Darling's emotions for the time being. Darling seemed completely unaware of the gravity of the situation, too absorbed in himself to notice the line he had crossed. I wondered how a man like him had managed to survive in a place like Pecos County for so long. Perhaps it was Barkley who had helped him along the way, guiding, supporting, and protecting him. But the arrival of Diane Barkley had created a rift between them.

"You're being too hasty," Barkley said. "If you rush Diane, you'll ruin any chance of happiness with her. She might be won over, but if you tell her who I am, she'll hate you forever. She might marry you to save me, but she'll hate you for it."

"That's not an option," growled Darling. "The gang won't let us go. We can't just leave them behind."

"We could sell everything and leave the country," Barkley suggested. "That way, you'd have a chance with Diane."

"I told you, we have to stick with the gang," Darling insisted. "We can't go without their approval. We'd have to sacrifice everything."

"So, you mean we'd have to double-cross them?" Barkley asked. "Leave them behind to face whatever comes?"

"That's exactly what I mean," said Darling.

"I'm not that kind of man," Barkley replied. "If the gang won't let me go, I'll stay and face the consequences."

"Hey, have you ever noticed that most of our deals in the past few years have been yours?" asked Darling.

"Yeah, I know. If I hadn't brought them in, we wouldn't have had any at all. Owens says you've been getting cold feet lately, especially since Ranger Foster arrived," replied Barkley.

"Call it cold feet if you want, but I call it common sense. We reached our limit a while ago. We started small, rustling a few cattle when it was still a joke. But as our greed grew, so did our boldness. Then came the gang, the regular trips, and before we knew it, we had shady deals, hold-ups, and even murders on our record. And once we were in, we couldn't turn back," explained Darling.

"I think we've all said that before. None of us wants to quit. We all think we can't be caught. We might be blamed, but nothing can be proven. We're too strong," added Barkley.

"That's where you're wrong," said Barkley firmly. "I used to think that way too, not long ago. I was stubborn. Who would ever suspect Roger Barkley of being part of a rustler gang? But I've changed my mind. I've started thinking logically. We're crooked, and we can't keep this up. It's the nature of life, even here in wild Pecos, for things to get better. The smart thing for us to do would be to divide everything equally and leave the country, all of us."

"But you and I have all the stock and all the gains," protested Darling. "I'll split mine."

"I won't. That's final," replied Barkley. He spread his hands wide, as if to say there was no point in trying to convince Darling. Talking only seemed to agitate him more. A dangerous glint shone in his eyes. "Your stock and property will only do you good until Foster--"

"Bah!" interrupted Darling, his voice hoarse. The mention of the Ranger's name was like a spark to a powder keg.

"You know that Ranger Foster is as good as dead, right?" said one man to the other. "Yeah, I remember you mentioning that," replied the second man sarcastically. "But tell me, how do you plan on making that happen?" "Blome is here to take care of it," said the first man confidently. "Bah!" scoffed the second man. "Blome doesn't stand a chance against Foster. No one on this border is quick and smart enough to take him down." "Why is that?" asked a third man, sullenly. "Because Foster is one of the best shots around," said the second man. "I've seen him draw his gun, and let me tell you, it's something to behold." "Well, if Jack doesn't kill him, I will," said the third man, pounding the table. The second man laughed contemptuously. "You're not thinking straight, Reuben. You've been on this border for ten years, and you think you can take down Foster? You're not even close to being on his level." The third man cursed in amazement, his emotions getting the better of him. "Barkley, I don't like your talk," he said. "Well, if you don't like it, you know what you can do," replied the second man bluntly. "I'm sick of this mess, and frankly, I wouldn't care if Foster took down some of us."

He stood up, his demeanor cool and collected, his eyes flashing with danger. "Look, that's not important," said Darling, clearly intimidated by the other man. "What matters is, do I get the girl?" "Only if she consents," replied Barkley, his voice low and cold.

"You won't force her to marry me?" "No. No," Barkley responded firmly. "Fine. Then I'll make her," Darling threatened. Barkley clearly understood the situation and didn't waste any more words. I knew that Barkley had a gun within reach and was prepared to use it. Suddenly, heavy footsteps sounded outside on the porch. It may have been my imagination, but I believed those footsteps saved Darling's life. "They're here," said Darling, opening the door. Five masked men entered the room. I recognized Blome by his fair skin and hair, his clothing, and his distinguished air. The men were all wearing coats, concealing any weapons they may have had. The big man with broad shoulders shook hands with Barkley, and the others hung back. The atmosphere in the room had shifted. Darling seemed to be insignificant, while Barkley was a different man altogether, a stranger to me. Any hope he may have had of escaping his gang and finding safety in another country vanished at the sight of these men. There was power in their presence, and he was trapped. The big man spoke in low, hoarse whispers, and the others huddled around him at the table. There were signs of membership that were not clear to me. The men bent their heads together, speaking in low voices, asking questions, answering, arguing. I strained to hear a word here and there.

The group was deep in planning, and I didn't dare try to decipher their words just yet. I made a mental note of everything I heard, knowing I could piece it all together later. As the rustlers wrapped up their discussion, my mind was racing and I couldn't keep up. I broke out in a cold sweat when I heard that Foster was to be killed by Blome or the gang at his home that very night. Morton was also a target, to be dealt with by Bo Snecker. Anyone else associated with Foster or suspected of being a threat was to be silenced, and violence would be unleashed on the town to intimidate the locals who were starting to question the Ranger's authority. After that, they planned to rustle herds of stock from nearby ranches and drive them to El Paso. The leader of the group, who I later identified as Snecker, left quickly with his son. The rest of the group stayed for a friendly chat with Barkley, smoking cigars and drinking liquor. Blome was charming and talkative, while Darling kept to himself, smoking and drinking steadily.

Suddenly, he stood up straight, as if he had heard something. "What's that?" he called out. The talking and laughter stopped. I strained my ears and heard a faint rustling sound. "It must be a rat," Barkley said in relief. It was strange how sudden or unknown things weighed on him. The rustling turned into a rattle. "Sounds like a rattlesnake to me," Blome said. Barkley got up from the table and looked around the room. Just then, I felt a slight movement of the adobe wall behind me. I could hardly believe my senses. But the rattle inside Barkley's room mixed with the sound of dirt falling. The adobe wall, made of dried mud, was crumbling. I felt a tremor pass through it. Then the blood rushed back to my heart, making me feel sick. "What the hell!" Barkley exclaimed. "I smell dust," Blome said sharply. That was my signal to drop down from my hiding spot, but I made a noise despite my efforts. "Did you hear a step?" Barkley asked. Then a section of the wall fell inward with a crash. I began to squeeze my body through the narrow passage toward the patio. "Hear him!" Darling yelled. "Over here!" "No, he's going that way," someone else yelled. The sound of heavy boots gave me the strength and speed of desperation. I wasn't avoiding a fight, but being cornered like a trapped coyote was another matter. I almost tore my clothes off in that passage. The dust almost choked me. When I burst into the patio, it was just in time. One deep breath revived me, and I stood up with my gun in hand, running for the exit to the court. Thumping footsteps made me turn back. I didn't want to face the odds in a fight when there was a chance to escape. I thought I heard someone running into the patio from the other end.

I crept forward, not sure where the door would take me. Gently, I nudged it open and slipped inside.

Chapter Nine.

As I entered the room, a soft moan caught my attention. The space was brightly lit, and there sat Gwen Langdon, wrapped in her dressing gown, on the edge of her bed. I pointed my gun at her, signaling her to remain silent, and turned to shut the door. The door was a sturdy one, but it lacked any bolt or bar, making me feel only marginally safer. I scanned the room, and my gaze rested on the window, the blinds pulled tight. Straining my ears, I heard the sound of fading footsteps, and then I turned to look at Gwen. She had fallen to her knees, her hands shaking in front of her as if to plead for mercy and protect herself. Her face was ashen, and her fear was palpable. I gestured for her to remain quiet and moved towards her, intent on calming her down. "Tim! Tim!" she whispered frantically, and I feared she might faint. As I drew closer and looked into her eyes, I realized the dark expression in them. She believed I had come to harm her, or worse, and I knew she had heard many unflattering stories about me, yet she had cared for me regardless. I recollected that she had broken her promise, had led me to kiss her, and had made a fool out of me. I also remembered the threats I had made to her. This intrusion was my way of taking revenge as a wild cowboy. I imagined she thought I was drunk, judging by my harsh and rugged appearance, and in an attempt to reassure her, I placed my gun on her dresser. "You poor thing," I whispered, attempting to lift her up.

But she remained on her knees, clinging to me. "Tim! That was awful of me," she whispered. "I know it. I deserve anything, anything! But I'm just a kid. Tim, I didn't break my promise. I didn't make you kiss me just for vanity's sake. I swear I didn't. I wanted you to. Because I care, Tim, I can't help it. Please forgive me. Please let me go this time. Don't, don't--"

"Will you shut up!" I interrupted, half out of my mind. I used force in another way than words. I shook her and sat her on the bed. "You little fool, I didn't come here to harm you or do something terrible, as you think. For God's sake, Gwen, what do you take me for?"

"Tim, you swore you'd do something awful if I tempted you again," she faltered. The way she searched my face with doubtful, fearful eyes hurt me.

"Listen," and with that, I felt a sense of peace. "I didn't know this was your room. I came in here to escape and save my life. I was being chased. I was spying on Barkley and his men. They heard me, but they didn't see me. They don't know who was listening. They're after me now. I'm Special United States Deputy Marshal Sittell Timell Archibald Sittell. I'm a Ranger. I'm here as secret aid to Foster."

Gwen's eyes changed from blank voids to widening, darkening, quickening windows of thought. "Tim-ell Archi-bald Sittell," she repeated. "Ranger! Secret aid to Foster!"

"Yes."

"Then you're not a cowboy?"

"No."

"Just pretending to be one?"

"Yes."

"And the drinking, gambling, and association with those low men--that was all an act?"

"Part of the game, Gwen. I'm not a drinking man. And I sure hate those places I had to go to and all that goes with them."

"Oh, so that's it! I knew there was something."

Gwen threw her arms around my neck, exclaiming how glad she was. She kissed me and showed her love without any reservation. It was a moment of pure joy for her, as she felt vindicated that I was not disreputable. She was entirely different from how she had ever been before. There was a moment of sweet confusion, where we both met halfway in tenderness. Suddenly, she began to cry, and I whispered in her ear to be careful as my life was at stake. She cried silently with her head on my breast and her hand holding mine. I held her for what seemed like a long time, and I could hear indistinct voices and footsteps in the distance. The wind rustled the rose-bush outside, and I heard a rider mounting for some reason. With my life at stake, I savored the sweetness of the situation. Gwen stirred in my arms, raised her tear-stained yet happy face, and tried to smile. She whispered that it wasn't the right time to cry, but she had to. She couldn't understand what it meant to her to learn that I was no drunkard or desperado, but a man like that Ranger. She kissed me again and said that if she didn't love me honestly and truly before, she did now. Then she stood up, with the fire and intelligence of a woman in her eyes, and asked me if I had been spying on her uncle. I told her briefly what had happened before I entered her room, not leaving out any details about the character of the men I had watched.

"Oh no, you don't!" Gwen exclaimed, grabbing my arm and pulling me back. "You're staying right here, Tim. I won't let you leave and get hurt. We'll wait until it's safe."

I couldn't argue with her determination. She was right, it was too risky to try and escape now. So I nodded and sat down on the edge of her bed. Gwen turned off the lamp, leaving us in darkness.

We sat quietly for what felt like hours, listening to the sounds of the house. Every creak and rustle made me jump, thinking it was someone coming to find me. But Gwen remained calm, reassuring me that we were safe.

Eventually, the noises stopped and the house fell silent. "Okay, Tim," Gwen whispered. "I think it's clear now. You can go."

I stood up and she handed me a flashlight. "Thanks, Gwen," I said gratefully. "You saved my life."

She smiled at me in the dim light. "Just be careful out there, Tim. And come back to me when you can."

I nodded and crept out of her room, making my way through the dark house towards the back door. As I slipped out into the night, I knew I had to get as far away from that place as possible. But I also knew I couldn't leave Gwen behind. I had to find a way to come back and rescue her too.

Her embrace was enough to weaken even the strongest of men. As I touched the chair, my knees buckled and I was grateful to sit down. I was covered in sweat, and a cold shiver ran through me. I thought I was losing my nerve. The proof of Gwen's love for me was so sweet and overwhelming that I couldn't resist, even if it meant saving her from disgrace.

"Tim, just being here will save you if they come," Gwen whispered softly. "I don't care what they think." She wrapped her arms around my neck, and I held her as if she were my only hope. Suddenly, we were interrupted by a noise. A stealthy sound, a step. We froze, our embrace turning to stone.

"Up yet, Gwen?" came Barkley's voice, too strained and eager to be natural.

"No, I'm in bed reading. Good night, Uncle," Gwen replied calmly and naturally. I marveled at the difference between man and woman. Perhaps that was the difference between love and hate.

"Are you alone?" Barkley asked, his voice now colder.

"Yes," Gwen replied.

The door swung open with a swift scrape and jar. Barkley half-entered, haggard and flaming-eyed. His gun was leveled at me, and behind him, I saw Darling and another man, indistinctly.

"Well!" Barkley gasped. He showed amazement. "Hands up, Tim!"

I put up my hands quickly, but I was calculating my chances of leaping for my gun or dashing out the light. I was trapped, and fury bit into me like the hot teeth of a wolf. The leveled gun, the menace in Barkley's puzzled eyes, Darling's dark and hateful face, all loosened the spirit of fight in me.

If Gwen hadn't been there, I might have done something foolish. Barkley was blocking Darling from entering, which showed he was both in control and distrustful. "You lied!" Barkley accused Gwen. He was as hard as flint, yet also uncertain and curious. "Of course I lied," Gwen replied, almost flippantly. She was cool and collected, and I realized she was a force to be reckoned with in this situation. Suddenly, she stepped between Barkley and me. "Move aside," Barkley ordered sternly. "I won't!" Gwen refused. "I don't care about your stupid gun. You're not going to shoot Tim or do anything else to him. It's my fault he's here in my room. I asked him to come."

"You little hussy!" Barkley exclaimed, lowering his gun. If I ever had reason to admire Gwen before, I certainly did then. She showed no fear and looked like she could fight like a tigress. She was calm, defiant, and white as a sheet. "How long has Tim been here?" Barkley demanded. "All evening. I left Diane at eight o'clock. Tim came right after that," Gwen answered.

"But you were undressed for bed!" Barkley was angry and perplexed. "Yes," Gwen replied simply. Her answer was so noncommittal, so innocent, and yet so confounding that Barkley just stared at her in astonishment. I started to speak passionately, but Gwen whirled into my arms and covered my mouth with her hand. "It's my fault. I'll take the blame," she cried. The fear in her voice made me realize it was wise to stay quiet.

"Uncle," Gwen began, turning her head but still holding onto me, "I've teased Tim into loving me. I've flirted with him, tempted him, and now we're engaged. Please, please don't..." She started to falter, and I felt her weight sag against me. "Let go of him," Barkley said.

"I ain't gonna hurt him, Gwen. How long y'all been foolin' around?" I asked."For weeks, I reckon. I don't rightly know," Gwen replied."Does Diane know?""She knows we love each other, but she don't know about this," Gwen said.Suddenly, we heard the sound of footsteps and rustling silk. Barkley spoke up, "Is that you, Reuben?"Miss Barkley's voice could be heard, "What's all this commotion? I hear--""Diane, go back," Barkley interrupted.Miss Barkley's beautiful face appeared beside Darling. She saw all of us and exclaimed, "Papa! Gwen!"Barkley laughed, and Gwen looked like she was about to faint. I couldn't lie to Miss Barkley for Gwen's sake. Darling spoke up, "Diane, your father and I interrupted a little Romeo and Juliet scene."Miss Barkley's gaze swept from Reuben to her father, then to Gwen's attire and her shamed face, and finally to me."Tim, they insinuating you came to Gwen's room?" she asked.Gwen confessed and said, "Diane, I told you I loved him, didn't I?""It's a--" I started to say before Gwen fainted. I caught her and Miss Barkley hurried to her side. Barkley said, "Tim, your hand's called."

"You can swear all you want, but we both know the truth now. Save your breath," I said, eyeing the man in front of me with a mix of contempt and amusement. "If it weren't for Gwen sticking up for you, I would have shot you on the spot."

I grabbed my gun from the bureau and holstered it, preparing to leave. But I couldn't resist stealing one last glance at Miss Barkley. Despite her scornful expression, I could see the sadness in her eyes. It was clear that she needed friends, but her misplaced trust had left her bitter and alone.

As I walked out the door, I couldn't help but feel a twinge of sympathy for her. I knew that what hurt her the most was the deep sorrow she was trying to conceal. But I had a job to do, and sentimentality had no place in the harsh world of the Wild West.

Chapter Ten.

As I stepped out into the darkness, the cool wind against my hot face brought a sense of relief, mixed with other emotions. Barkley had suggested that I leave the ranch, and while I didn't take it as a dismissal, I knew it would be wise to depart at once. Even if my footprints were hidden by the daylight, my work there was done. So I gathered my few belongings and headed to my room. The night was dark, windy, and stormy, but no rain fell. I hoped that leaving the ranch would ease the pain I felt, but the lump in my throat and the ache in my chest persisted long after I'd left the ranch behind.

My thoughts were consumed by Gwen, a game and loyal little girl who'd surprised me with her steadfastness. What would the future hold for us? I had no clue, but I held onto a vague hope that once the trouble was over, there might be something more between us.

I arrived at our rendezvous point among the rocks, but Foster was nowhere in sight. The hour was late, and I knew I'd have to wait until morning to see him.

Amidst the few dim lights flickering on the outskirts of town, I spotted the glow of his small adobe house. However, I knew with almost complete certainty that he was not there. So, I made my way into the darkness, not expecting to find Foster but intending to find a safe place to stay until morning. There was no path, and the night was so black that I could only see the lighter patches of sandy ground. I stumbled over small clumps of brush, fell into washes, and pricked myself on cacti. As I traveled further, mesquites and rocks made my journey even more challenging. Eventually, I found myself on higher ground and felt a sense of familiarity with the surroundings. I knew I was likely near Foster's hiding spot. I continued to move forward until rocks and brush blocked my path, and I attempted to whistle, but there was no response. I spread my blanket in a sheltered spot and went to sleep. The coyotes were howling, and the wind was rushing through the mesquites, but I slept through it all. I woke up to discover that a little rain had fallen during the night, but it was not enough to cause me any discomfort. The morning was bright and beautiful, but I was not in the mood to enjoy it. I had work to do that did not match the golden wave of grass and brush on the windy plain. I climbed up to the highest rock on the ridge and surveyed the area. It was a wild location, roughly three miles from town. I recognized landmarks that Foster had given me and knew I was close to his hideout. I whistled and called out, but there was no reply. However, by traversing the ridge back and forth, I eventually found a faint trail.

I followed the trail, losing it and finding it again. Eventually, I climbed higher up another ridge and found Foster's hideout. He had been gone for at least two days. I wondered where he had slept. I found a pack of food protected by a heavy slab under a shelving rock. There was also a canteen full of water. I quickly ate some breakfast and hid my own pack before setting off at a rapid pace towards town.

However, my journey was interrupted when I spotted two cowboys on horseback. They seemed to be searching for something. I became suspicious and watched them closely before following them for a mile or so. Eventually, I was satisfied they were not tracking Foster. It took a long time for them to disappear from view, so I waited before continuing my journey.

As I approached town, I noticed more horsemen on the flat. I lay low for a while and made a wide detour to avoid being seen. It was already afternoon when I finally arrived in town. I couldn't explain why, but I felt that something had happened since my last visit. I was curious and anxious.

The first person I saw was Dick. He handed me a note from Gwen. She assumed that I had left the ranch and forgiven my deceit. Gwen had softened towards me when she learned that we were engaged. She asked me to meet her that night at eight in a secluded spot among the trees and shrubbery. It was a brief note, but it got straight to the point.

The situation had a strange effect on me. I had thought the engagement was just a spur-of-the-moment idea, but now that I was safe, Gwen wouldn't have continued with the charade just to impress Miss Barkley. No, she was serious about it. If I played my cards right, I could still have her. But what was the right thing to do? I was torn and deeply moved. It was difficult to put her out of my mind. I decided to head to Foster's house, but he wasn't there.

The lamp was out, and the oil was low. There were several tracks around, but I couldn't tell which were Foster's. As I left, I noticed some of his neighbors watching me from their windows and doors.

Next, I went to Mrs. Dempsey's house. She was up and about, and the children were happy and cared for. She hadn't seen Foster since I had last seen him. It was clear that the worst was over for her, and she was determined to face the future with hope. From there, I headed to the main street of Linrock, where violence was always looming. Surprisingly, the street was quiet, and there were only a few people around. The entire block was lined with saddled horses. I entered the Hope So barroom and was taken aback by how full it was, yet how quiet it seemed.

The entire bar was filled with men wearing rolled-up sleeves, slouched hats, and flapping vests. Some were drinking while others spoke in hushed tones. Several dusty tables held groups of motley men, some silent while others spoke and gestured earnestly. I scanned the crowd but didn't see anyone I was particularly interested in. The main players in my drama were nowhere to be found. However, there were more rough characters present than I had ever seen before. Their voices were too low for me to hear, but I followed the direction of their significant gestures. That's when I noticed that the half dozen tables were closely grouped and drawn back from the center of the room. My quick eyes then took in a smashed table and chairs, broken bottles on the floor, and a dark, sinister splotch of blood. I didn't have time to ask any questions because Frank Morton caught my eye in the doorway and wanted to get my attention. He turned away and I followed him outside where he was leaning against the hitching-rail. One look at him and I could tell that he knew about my involvement in Foster's game, and that he was ready to fight. He had a clouded brow, looked somber and thick, and seemed slow and guarded. "Howdy, Tim," he said. "We've been wanting you." "There's ten of us in town, all scattered around, ready. It's going to start today." "Where's Foster?" I asked. "Saw him less than an hour ago. He's somewhere close. He may show up anytime." "Is he all right?" "Well, he was pretty fit a little while back," replied Morton significantly. "What's happened? Tell me everything." "Well, the ball started rolling last night, I reckon. Jack Blome came swaggering in here asking for Foster. We all knew what he was in town for."

Last night, Blome made a scene. He shouted for the Ranger, and everyone in the saloons and on the streets heard him. His friends joined in, and they all had a good time. I asked if they drank heavily, but apparently, they didn't. They just laid the foundations. Foster wasn't around last night, but Blome and his gang were up early this morning. They traveled alone, and Blome walked up and down the street alone, thirty-one times. I counted them. From what I could tell, Blome didn't drink, but his gang, especially Bo Snecker, definitely did.

By eleven o'clock, everyone in town knew what was going on. There was no work or business, except in the saloons. Zimmer and I were together, and the rest of our group was in pairs at different places. Around noon, Blome got tired of parading and went into the Hope So, with the crowd following. Zimmer stayed outside to give Foster a hint if he showed up, and I went in to watch.

It was fascinating to me, and I've been in Texas my whole life. I'd never seen a gunman on the job before. Blome was handsome and seemed different from what I expected. I thought he'd be shouting and prancing around like a drunken fool, but he was cool and quiet enough. His friends were the ones doing the drinking and blowing. After a while, I realized that Blome was reveling in the situation. He wasn't like a dark, sullen, and restless man dead-set on killing someone. He was vain and cocksure, enjoying the effect he was making.

I knew exactly what kind of man Blome was. He sat on the edge of a table, facing the door. He had a partner outside, keeping an eye out for Foster. But Foster didn't come in that way. Zimmer told me that Foster wasn't on the street just before that time. He had to have been in the Hope So somewhere. But then, like magic, he appeared through the door near the bar. Blome didn't even notice him come in, but the rest of us did. The room went silent.

"Hello Blome, I hear you're looking for me," Foster called out. I don't know if he spoke normally or not, but his voice captivated me. And it seemed to have the same effect on Blome. The man turned gray, frozen in place. He was clearly trying to think, but it was difficult in that moment.

Blome slowly turned his head, expecting to be staring down the barrel of a gun. But Foster was just standing there in his shirt sleeves, hands on his hips. He looked like the most manly man I had ever seen. It's hard to describe the feeling he gave off, but it was powerful.

Blome was at a disadvantage. He was half-sitting on a table, and Foster was behind and to the left of him. Any sudden movements from Blome would have been foolish, and everyone knew it. The crowd slid back without making a sound, but Bo Snecker and a rustler named March stayed near Blome. I knew that Bo Snecker was just as dangerous as Blome, and I was proven right.

Foster didn't want to keep his advantage, though. He walked around in front of the rustler, not bothering to maintain his position.

As soon as Foster stepped in, the crowd shifted to face him. It seemed like he knew what he was doing. "I hear you've been looking for me," the Ranger repeated. Blome didn't move, but I could tell he was paying attention. Foster's presence seemed to have an effect on him that I hadn't seen before.

"Yes, I have," Blome finally replied. "Well, here I am. What do you want?"

Everyone in the room knew what Blome had wanted to do, but Foster's question still seemed odd. However, now that he was standing there, it made sense. "If you heard I was looking for you, you sure heard what for," Blome said.

"Blome, my experience with men like you is that you all talk a big game when I'm not around, but when I show up, you mean something else entirely. I've called you out now. What do you mean?" Foster responded.

"I reckon you know what Jack Blome means," Blome said.

"Jack Blome? That name means nothing to me. You've been going around bragging that you'd meet me and kill me. You thought you meant it, didn't you?" Foster challenged.

"Yes, I did mean it," Blome admitted.

"All right. Go ahead!" Foster said.

The barroom was dead silent. No one moved. Blome's face turned gray again, like stone. I thought, and I'm sure everyone else watching thought, that Blome was going to draw his gun and get himself killed. But he didn't. Foster had intimidated him. If Blome had been drunk or angry or anything but what he was at that moment, he might have pulled his gun. But he didn't. I'd heard of brave men getting scared like that, and after seeing Foster, I didn't blame Blome.

"You see, Blome, you don't really want to meet me, despite all your talk," Foster said. "You thought you did, but that was before you faced the man you intended to kill."

"You're one of those fancy, overconfident braggarts, Blome," Foster said, stepping forward. "I know because I've met real gunfighters, and they never talk like you do. So don't go around boasting anymore."

Blome got up and left the place, but as I turned my attention back to Foster, I heard a commotion. Foster had a hold of Bo Snecker, who was trying to pull out his gun. Snecker wasn't quick enough, and his gun went off in the air before Foster disarmed him. The table was overturned, and March, the other rustler, pulled his gun.

But before he could fire, someone in the crowd shot him down. No one saw who fired the shot, and the crowd scattered.

Foster dragged Snecker to jail and locked him up. That was the end of it for the day, but I knew Foster had opened a can of worms with his actions. I was ready to join in the game, but something was different this time. The thrill of danger wasn't as wild as it used to be.

"Morton, you mentioned someone else played a hand in this and killed March," I said.

"That's right," Morton replied. "It wasn't any of our men. Zimmer was outside."

The rest of the group was scattered about. "Foster has more friends than we thought," said one of the men. "It seems like it has the gang all riled up. Things are going to get crazy tonight." "Foster doesn't really expect to keep Snecker in jail, does he?" "I can't say for sure. Probably not. I wish Foster had taken care of both Blome and Snecker. We would have less of a fight on our hands." "Maybe. I prefer the elimination method myself. But Foster doesn't rely on guns. He only uses them as a last resort. It's hard to get him to draw. These dangerous men aren't afraid of guns or fights, but they are afraid of Foster. Maybe it's his nerve, the way he confronts them, the things he says, or the fact that he has help from mysterious allies." "Tim, we're all behind him. I bet the honest citizens of Linrock will support him soon. I can see it coming. Dempsey had a list of twenty or more men, but Foster didn't want that many." "We don't need more. Morton, do you have any idea where Foster is?" "No idea whatsoever." "Okay. I'll look for him. If you see him, tell him to lay low and then come find me. Tell him I've spotted our men." "Tim, you Rangers are amazing!" exclaimed Morton, his eyes shining. Foster didn't show up in town again that day. He was being cunning. By four o'clock that afternoon, Blome and his rustlers were drunk and causing trouble. They roamed the streets, shooting their guns, but I didn't see or hear of anyone getting hurt. The lawless element, both locals and visitors, followed Blome from saloon to saloon.

I had seen similar processions in many towns throughout wild Texas, though not on such a grand scale. In Linrock, whiskey and guns were the two great and dangerous things at this hour. Under such conditions, the rustlers were capable of any mad act of folly. Morton and his men spread word around town that a fight was imminent and all citizens should be prepared to defend their homes against possible violence. Despite his warning, I saw many respectable citizens abroad, whose quiet, unobtrusive manner and watchful eyes, along with their hard faces, told me that when trouble began, they wanted to be there.

Ranger Foster had built his house of service upon a rock, and the next few days, perhaps hours, would see a great change in the character and a proportionate decrease in number of the inhabitants of this corner of Pecos County. Morton and I were among the crowd that watched Blome, Snecker, and a dozen other rustlers march down to Foster's jail. They had crowbars and cans of giant powder that they had taken from a hardware store. If Foster had a jailer, he was not in sight. The door was wrenched off, and Bo Snecker, who was evidently not fully recovered, was brought forth to his cheering comrades.

Then, some of the rustlers began to urge back the pressing circle, and the word given out acted as a spur to their haste. The jail was to be blown up. The crowd split, and some men ran one way, while others ran another. Morton and I were among those who hurried over the vacant ground to a little ridge that marked the edge of the open country. From this vantage point, we heard several rustlers yell in warning, then they fled for their lives. It turned out that they might have spared themselves such headlong flight. The explosion appeared to be long in coming.

Eventually, we witnessed the roof of Foster's jail lift up in a cloud of red dust. A deep, low explosion followed shortly after. The thick dust settled, revealing only a portion of the stone walls that once made up the jail. The nearby adobe building was also badly damaged. Despite the destruction, Blome and his followers were not satisfied. They let out wild yells and huzzahs as they used crowbars to bring down every stone of the jail. Snecker led the way as they marched up the town. It was clear that this was a gang in the mood for evil or ridiculous celebration.

Although the crowd dispersed and disappeared from the streets of Linrock, the impression they left behind was that they were content. However, Morton and I were convinced that there was still devilry afoot. I assured him that I would see Foster early in the evening and that we would be safe. Morton promised to keep a sharp eye on Blome's gang during the night.

As the sun began to set, I stopped by the Hope So for a quick bite and drink before my meeting with Gwen. On my way out, I passed by a dark street until I reached the end where, strangely enough, Foster's house was illuminated. I walked past it and whistled low, even though I knew he wouldn't be there. I paused and waited, watching as a long, dark shadow moved across the windows.

If it weren't for Foster's clever shadow trick, I would've been fooled. He expected his house to be attacked at night while he was home, but didn't think he needed to stick around to make sure. Criminals like these were often simple and easy to deceive. I made my way across the open area, avoiding any obvious paths, towards Barkley's house on the hill. It was dark under the trees, and I struggled to find the secluded spot where I was supposed to wait for Gwen. I trusted her to find it though. She might be nervous, but she was dependable.

As I sat down to wait, I heard rustling and footsteps, and Gwen emerged from the darkness. She came straight into my arms, and it was a sweet moment. I had forgotten in the midst of all the chaos that she would do just this. I expected her to be emotional, but she surprised me.

"Tim, are you okay?" she whispered.

"Just fine at the moment," I replied. Gwen hugged me again before sitting down beside me.

"I can only stay for a minute," she said. "But it's safe. I told Diane I was meeting you and she's waiting to hear about Foster."

"He's safe for now," I interrupted. "There were people coming and going all day. Uncle Roger didn't show up for meals and Reuben was pacing and drinking."

We heard him roar that someone had been shot and we feared it might be Foster. "No," I replied calmly, "Did Foster shoot anyone?" "No. A rustler named March tried to draw on Foster, and someone in the crowd killed March." "Someone? Tim, was it you?" I asked suspiciously. "It sure wasn't. I wasn't there," he replied. "Ah! Then Foster has other men like you around him. I might have guessed that," I said. "Gwen, Foster makes friends because he's on the side of justice," Tim explained. "Diane will be glad to hear that. She doesn't just think of Foster's life. I believe she has a secret pride in his work. And I have an idea that what she fears most is some kind of clash between Foster and her father," I said. "I shouldn't wonder. Gwen, what does Diane know about her father?" Tim asked. "Oh, she's in the dark. She got hold of some papers that made her ask him questions. His answers made her suspicious. She realizes he's not what he has pretended to be all these years. But she never dreams her father is a rustler chief. When she finds that out..." I broke off, unable to finish the sentence. "Listen, Gwen," Tim said suddenly. "I have an idea that Foster's house will be attacked by the gang tonight, and destroyed, same as the jail was this afternoon. These rustlers are crazy. They'll expect to kill him while he's there. But he won't be there. If you and Diane hear shooting and yelling tonight, don't be frightened. Foster and I will be safe." "Oh, I hope so. Tim, I must hurry back. But, first, can't you arrange a meeting between Diane and Foster? It's her wish. She begged me to. She must see him," I said. "I'll try," Tim promised, knowing that promise would be hard to keep. "We could ride out from the ranch somewhere. You remember we used to rest on the high ridge where there was a shady place with such a beautiful outlook?"

"Don't worry about it, my dear. I remember where it was," Gwen said with a soft chuckle. She always seemed to find humor even in the most dismal situations. "Just tie your red scarf on that tall mesquite branch tomorrow morning, or the next, or any morning soon. I'll check with my binoculars every day. If I see the scarf, Diane and I will come out to you."

"Sounds like a plan, Gwen. You always have something up your sleeve," I replied with a smile. "Once upon a time, I thought your head was empty," I added jokingly. Gwen put a hand over my mouth.

"I have to go now," she said, standing up. She came close to me and wrapped her arms around my neck. "There's one more thing, Tim. It was hard to tell Diane that we're engaged. I had to lie to Uncle. What else could I have said to her? I-"

"Gwen, you lied to Barkley to save me. But you wouldn't have told Diane the truth if you hadn't already accepted my proposal," I interrupted.

"Oh, Tim, I've had you in my heart for so long. But it's been a while since you asked me, and I thought-"

"You thought I might have changed my mind? No, Gwen. I still want to make you my wife," I declared.

Gwen moved closer to me, and I could feel her feminine curves pressing against me. I held back, teasing myself with the thought of kissing her. "Gwen, do you love me?" I asked.

"More than anything. Since the first time I laid eyes on you," she confessed.

"I'm a marshal, a Ranger like Foster. I hunt down criminals and sometimes have to use force. It's a rough life, and there's always the possibility of getting hurt or killed. Are you sure you want to be my wife?" I asked, wanting to make sure she understood the risks.

"Oh, Tim! Yes, I'll be your wife. But when your duty is done here, I have some news for you. I'm an orphan, but I'm not poor. I own a plantation in Louisiana, and I want to make you a planter," Gwen revealed with a smile.

"Wow, Gwen! You're rich?" I exclaimed. "I'm afraid I am. But no one can say you married me for my money," she replied. "Well, no, not if you heard about my desperate attempts to win your heart when I thought you were a poor relative on a visit. My God! Gwen, if only I could successfully complete this Ranger job," I sighed. "You will," she reassured me with a gentle touch.

I then took a ring off my finger and placed it on hers. "That was my sister's. She's passed away now, and no other girl has ever worn it. Let it be your engagement ring. Gwen, I pray that I can make it through this challenging Ranger mission to make you happy and to become worthy of you!" I declared.

"Tim, I'm worried about one thing," Gwen whispered. "What's that?" I asked. "There will be fighting. And I saw into your eyes the other night when you stood with your hands up. You would kill anybody, Tim. It's terrifying! But don't think of me as weak. I understand what your job entails and the kind of man you must be. I can love you and stand by you, but if you killed a blood relative of mine, I would have to let you go. I'm a Southerner, and family is everything. I despise my uncle and cousin Reuben, but I love you. Please promise me that you will do everything possible to avoid that," she pleaded.

I was speechless, and we held each other tightly for a few moments, our lips locked in a passionate kiss. Then she abruptly pulled away, said a quick goodbye, and vanished into the night like a shadow. An hour later, I lay under the stars in the same spot where Foster and I always met. He was with me, but he had his face buried in his hands while I gazed up at the sky.

As I handed over the evidence of Diane Barkley's father's guilt to Foster, he had only one thing to say. "I wish I had called in someone who would have messed it up!" Although it was a compliment to me, it was obvious that Foster had hit rock bottom. I had no empathy left to offer him, as I was dealing with my own troubles. I couldn't shake off the memory of Gwen's embrace and the sensation of her lips on mine. I could only imagine the agony that Foster was going through. Time passed by slowly, as the sky turned dark blue and the stars sparkled brighter. The wind grew stronger and colder, and I could hear the sound of sand hitting the stones like the rustle of silk. It was an eerily quiet night, and I longed for the howling of the coyotes. Suddenly, a prairie wolf sent out a mournful cry from the distant ridges, and it sent shivers down my spine. The sound was so hauntingly tragic that it seemed to resonate with my own troubles. I waited for the sound to come again, but it was silent. Foster lay motionless, like a stone next to me. I wondered if he would ever speak. I even felt a petulant desire for him to sympathize with me. Just as I was checking the time, I heard a gunshot that shattered the silence. I jumped up and looked over the stone, and Foster stood up beside me, gasping for breath.

Chapter Eleven.

I could clearly spot the lights emanating from his adobe house, but naturally, nothing else was perceptible. There weren't any other illuminated residences in close proximity.

Multiple flashes illuminated the night sky before quickly fading, followed by the sounds of gunshots and the unmistakable sound of breaking glass. "Looks like those fools have started shooting, Foster," I said. Foster grunted in response, clearly still angry. I figured it was for the best that things had started happening - Foster needed to be shaken up. Suddenly, a sharp yell rang out, followed by a massive burst of light and a cloud of smoke or dust. Then, darkness descended, followed by a deep, thunderous boom. The lights in the house went out, and then there was a loud crash. Points of light appeared in a half-circle, and the sounds of guns mixed with the furious yells of men. All of this was drowned out by the roar of an angry mob. Another explosion, even heavier than the last, lit up the darkness and then tore through the air. It was followed by a continuous volley of yells, screams, and cheers that blended together to form a hideous roar of hatred. Even after it was clear that there was no possibility of anyone surviving under the ruins of the house, the noise persisted. It wasn't just hate for

Foster - it was a violent, lawless expression of anger directed at the Ranger Service. Similar events had happened in Texas and other states before, but they never seemed to occur more than once in the same area - perhaps they were events that could only happen once. I watched Foster throughout the entire ordeal, a manifestation of insane rage at his life and joy at his death, and when everything finally fell silent and he turned to look at me with his pale face, I felt a sense of dread. Dread was something that I was not used to feeling. "Looks like Blome and the Sneckers think they've got you, huh?" I said. "It'll be a pleasant surprise for them tomorrow, won't it, old man?"

"Tomorrow? Look, Tim, what's left of my old adobe house is on fire. The ruins won't be able to be searched anytime soon."

I made sure everything in my home was in place, trying to create the illusion that I was still there. I just wanted to give the rustlers a chance to fall for my trick. It's unbelievable how easily men like them can be fooled, especially when they're whiskey-soaked. They'll be in for a surprise!

I stood there a while, watching the fire smolder and the smoke curl up against the dark blue sky. "Tim, do you think they heard up at the ranch and think I'm-"

"They heard, of course," I interrupted. "But the girls know you're safe with me."

"Safe? I almost wish to God I was there under that heap of ruins, where the rustlers think they've left me."

"Well, Foster, old buddy, let's get some rest." With Foster leading the way, we walked out into the open.

Two days later, in the middle of the morning, I sat on a large, flat rock in the shade of a bushy mesquite tree. I gazed out at the vast, clear plain below, enjoying the view. Gwen sat as close to me as possible, holding onto my arm tightly as if she never wanted to let go. On the other side, Miss Barkley leaned against me, looking white and breathless, partly from the quick ride from the ranch, and partly from agitation. She had lost weight, and there were dark circles under her eyes, but she looked even more beautiful than before. The red scarf I had used to signal the girls waved from a branch of the mesquite tree. Their horses were parked at the foot of the ridge in a shady spot.

"Take off your hat," I told Gwen. "You look hot. Besides, you're prettier with your hair down." When she didn't move, I took it off for her, then did the same for Miss Barkley. She smiled faintly, thanking me. She had clearly forgotten all her resentment, and there were little beads of sweat on her forehead.

Her hair was a beautiful combination of black and brown, with strands of red and gold intertwined. I had orchestrated this meeting, and soon enough she would be leaning over Foster. I didn't care what he might do to me. There was an impending interview that would shake us all to our core, and my heart was heavy with the weight of it. However, I found solace in being in the open air with the girls once again. They were both quiet, which made it difficult for me to keep up my cheerful demeanor. In my eagerness to deflect any questions and appear happy for their sake, I ended up making a fool of myself with my silly banter and familiarity. I couldn't help but wonder if any Ranger had ever been in such a predicament.

"Diane, did Gwen show you her engagement ring?" I asked, determined to keep the conversation going. Miss Barkley didn't seem to mind my use of her first name. She appeared friendly and wistful. "Yes, it's very pretty. An antique. I've seen a few of them," she replied. "I hope you'll let Gwen marry me soon."

"Let her? Gwen Langdon? You haven't gotten to know your fiancée yet. But when-"

"Oh, next week, just as soon-"

"Tim!" Gwen interrupted, her face turning red.

"What's the matter?" I asked innocently. "You're a little ahead of yourself."

"Well, Gwen, I don't want to split hairs over dates. But you've become much more desirable in the light of certain revelations. Diane, wasn't Gwen quite deceitful? She's an heiress all this time! And I'm supposed to be a planter who smokes fine cigars and drinks mint juleps! But there won't be any juleps," I joked.

"Tim, you're talking nonsense," Gwen reprimanded. "This is no time to be funny."

"Alright," I replied, resigned. I discarded my hollow mask of humor. A silence hung in the air, and I waited for someone to break it.

"Is Foster alright?" Miss Barkley asked, concern etched on her face.

"He's not too bad," replied the man. "He's got a scalp wound where a bullet grazed him, but it's just a scratch. And then he has another in his shoulder, but it's not too serious."

"Where is he now?" she inquired.

"He's over on the other ridge. Look for the big white stone and you'll see our camp. He's resting there."

"When can I see him?" she asked, her voice quivering.

"He's asleep right now. He was up late due to the pain in his head. Let him rest for a bit longer and then you can see him."

"Did he know I was coming?" she asked, hopeful.

"No, he had no idea. He'll be happy to see you, but he's not too keen on seeing me," the man chuckled.

"Why's that?" she inquired.

"He's scared to see you. It makes his duty harder," he explained.

"Oh," she sighed, seeming to understand.

I couldn't help but ask, "Gwen, do you and Diane know what happened in town yesterday?"

"We don't know much," she replied. "Reuben was acting crazy and Uncle was cursing him. We heard rumors of fighting, but we don't know the details. Foster was apparently killed multiple times and then brought back to life."

I felt a tug on my heartstrings as I realized the gravity of the situation. The sooner they were reunited, the better.

When I saw the red scarf flapping in the wind this morning, I was overcome with relief. It meant Foster was safe and sound, or else the signal wouldn't have been raised. "Not many folks in Linrock know what really happened," I remarked to Tim with a wry chuckle.

Suddenly, Miss Barkley piped up. "Tell me about Foster and what he did yesterday," she implored earnestly.

I was taken aback. "Are you sure you want to know? It's not exactly a tale for delicate ears," I cautioned.

"I'm no coward," she retorted, her eyes flashing with determination.

"But why do you want to hear it all?" I pressed. I needed a good reason to dredge up the memories of that harrowing day.

She hesitated for a moment, then fixed her gaze on Foster, who was sleeping nearby. "I want to hear because I admire his work," she declared. It was clear from the fervor in her voice and the light on her face that there was more to it than just admiration.

"His work?" I echoed, incredulous. "Do you want him to succeed?"

"With all my heart," she replied, her face glowing with passion.

I couldn't help but exclaim, "My God!" and Gwen's fingers dug into my arm like sharp claws. I bit my tongue to keep from saying more. What if Foster had heard her confession?

Oh, how noble and just this blind girl was! But she knew even less than I had expected. I pushed my thoughts to the matter at hand. She reveled in the Ranger's work, hoping with all her heart that he would succeed. Her womanly pride swelled at his manliness. Maybe with a woman's intricate and incomprehensible motives, she desired to see Foster in all his power, the power that made him hated and feared by lawless men. Finally, she had accepted the wild life of the border as something terrible and inevitable, but passing. Foster was one of the strange, great, and misunderstood men who were making that wild life pass. For the first time, I realized that Miss Barkley, through the sharpened eyes of love, saw Foster for who he was, a wonderful and necessary violence. Her intelligence and sympathy had allowed her to see beyond defamation and false records that followed a Ranger. She had no choice but to love him. A woman's glory in a work that freed men, saved women, and made children happy effaced forever the horror of a few dark deeds of blood.

"Miss Barkley, I must tell you first," I hesitated. "That I'm not a cowboy. My wild stunts, my drinking, and gaming were all pretense."

"Indeed! I am very glad to hear it. Was Gwen in your confidence?" Miss Barkley asked.

"Only recently. I am a United States deputy marshal in Foster's service," I replied.

She gave a slight start but did not raise her head. "I have deceived you. But, all the same, I've been your friend. I ask you to respect my secret a little while. I'm telling you because otherwise, my relation to Foster yesterday would not be plain. Now, if you and Gwen will use this blanket, make yourselves more comfortable seats, I'll begin my story."

Miss Barkley allowed me to arrange a place for her where she could rest at ease, but Gwen returned to my side and stayed there.

Today, she was a mystery. Pale, brooding, and silent, she never looked at me unless my face was half turned away. I began to speak, "Night before last, Foster and I were hidden among the rocks near the edge of town. We watched as his house was destroyed. Foster had left the lights on, shadows moving across the window blinds, and a dummy in his bed. He even arranged for guns to go off inside the house if anyone tried to enter. All of this was to gain evidence against his enemies. It was not pleasant to wait and listen to that drunken mob of about a hundred men. The disturbance and intent worked strangely upon Foster. It made him different. In the dark, I couldn't tell how he looked, but I felt a mood coming from him that made me dread the next day.

About midnight, we started for our camp. Foster managed to get some sleep, but I couldn't. I was cold and hot by turns, eager and backward, furious and thoughtful. The deal was so complicated, and tomorrow was certainly nearing the climax. By morning, I was sick, distraught, gloomy, and uncertain. I had breakfast ready when Foster awoke. I hated to look at him, but when I did, it was like being revived.

He said, "Tim, you'll trail alongside me today and through the rest of this mess." That gave me another shock. I want to explain to you girls that this was the first time in my life I was backward at the prospect of a fight. The shock was the jump of my pulse. My nerve came back. To line up with Foster against Blome and his gang, that would be great!

"All right, old man," I replied. "We're going after them, then?"

He only nodded. After breakfast, I watched him clean, oil, and reload his guns. I didn't need to ask him if he expected to use them.

Without any hesitation, I followed Captain Neal's orders. Foster and I were to enter town together, but he planned to circle around and enter from the back of the Hope So. Meanwhile, I was to hurry ahead and post Morton and his men, gather intel on the gang, and be at the Hope So when Foster arrived.

I didn't need to ask if I could use my gun. I already intended to. We left camp and headed towards town. It was almost noon when we parted ways.

I approached town from the direction of Barkley's ranch. When I arrived, there was a crowd surrounding the ruins of Foster's house. It was nothing but a pile of crumbled adobe bricks and burnt logs, still smoking and hot. No one had attempted to dig through the rubble. The curious crowd was convinced that Foster was buried under the debris. One thing about the night assault stuck with me. Three rustlers were found dead in the daylight, killed by random shots. Others involved in the attack were also injured. I suspected that Morton and his men had taken advantage of the darkness and chaos to shoot some extra rounds that weren't part of the plan.

From there, I made my way to town. As I expected, Morton and Zimmer were hanging out in front of the Hope So, accompanied by some unsavory characters. At that point, Morton's gang hadn't come under suspicion. He was eager for news about Foster and when I told him the plan, he became as cool, dark, and grim as any man of my kind could have wished. He sent Zimmer to gather the others in their group. Then he shared a few details with me, but he didn't confirm or deny my suspicions about the three rustlers' deaths.

Blome, Bo Snecker, Hilliard, and Pickens, the ringleaders of the gang, were painting the town red to celebrate Foster's death.

Everyone at the party got drunk except for old man Snecker, who they teased for having cold feet. They were all too happy to pay attention to the old rustler's warnings or do any more shooting. The party lasted until two in the morning.

The next day, after eleven, Blome and his gang appeared one by one with their followers. The excitement had died down, and Ranger Foster was no longer in the way. Linrock was open and free again. However, Blome seemed sullen and unresponsive to his comrades and admirers. When I arrived, the whole gang, except for old man Snecker, was gathered in the Hope So saloon.

I asked Morton if Zimmer would be clever enough to bring his outfit in one or two at a time, and he reassured me. Then we went into the saloon. There were about sixty or seventy men inside, with more than half openly supporting Blome's gang. The rest were either of questionable character or secretly wanting to help any cause against the rustlers. I could tell from their shadowed faces, tense bodies, and overall unease. The windows were open, and the light was clear. Few men smoked, but all had a drink before them. The conversation was subdued, and I surveyed the scene, picking out a spot close to Foster when he entered.

Eventually, Zimmer and a man entered and went to the bar. Other men came and went, and Blome, Bo Snecker, Hilliard, and Pickens sat at a table in the light of the open windows. I recognized the faces of the last two, but Morton had to inform me of their names. Pickens was small, scrubby, dusty, sandy, and mottled, resembling a rattlesnake.

Hilliard was a towering figure, with a bronzed complexion, a massive mustache, and piercing, hollow eyes that gave off an intimidating aura. As soon as I laid eyes on him, I couldn't help but think that he looked like a grave-robber. Bo Snecker was a different story altogether. He was a lean, mean, hard-looking young man with a dangerous air about him, as if he was too wild and reckless to have any sense of caution or fear. And then there was Blome, who looked like he had just crawled out of a ditch somewhere. He used to be a handsome fellow, but now his face was swollen and discolored, and his eyes were clouded with shame and regret. He had tried to drown his sorrows in drink, but it hadn't worked. He knew that he had failed as a gunman, and that his reputation had been tarnished forever.

As we waited for Foster to arrive, the rest of the men milled around lazily, chatting and joking with each other. They were all still half-asleep, and didn't seem to realize the gravity of the situation. But I knew better. I knew that Foster was a master of surprise, and that he would catch them off-guard. I kept my eyes peeled for any signs of trouble, and tried to stay alert. But I couldn't help feeling sorry for poor Blome. I knew that his time was running out, and that he was about to face a swift and merciless Ranger who would show him no mercy.

In the end, it all happened so fast that I could barely keep up. Foster burst into the room like a whirlwind, and chaos erupted all around us. Blome was the first to go down, of course, but he wasn't the only one. The rest of the men fought back fiercely, but it was no use. Foster was too quick, too deadly, and too determined to let anyone escape. In the end, it was just me and him, standing alone amidst the carnage. I knew that I had to be careful, or I would end up like the rest of them. But I also knew that I had to take a stand, and fight for what I believed in. And so, with a heavy heart, I drew my gun and prepared to face my fate.

I knew that Foster had the ability to take out Blome's comrades at the table in the blink of an eye if he wanted to. My strategy was to keep an eye on his outside partners. This proved to be the right move, as it allowed me to save Foster's life.

As time passed, the Ranger still hadn't shown up and I began to feel uneasy. Could he have been stopped? I dismissed the thought. Who would have been able to stop him? The wait felt longer than it actually was, and the tension in the room was palpable. Morton was clearly feeling the pressure, and the other men looked strained and anxious, as if they were anticipating something terrible.

I caught Blandy's eye on me and I didn't like the look in it. I made a mental note to keep an eye on him. Blandy, the bartender at Hope So, was someone I didn't trust.

I paused to clear my throat and catch my breath. "He was," I replied ambiguously to Gwen's question. I didn't want to give away too much information just yet.

I kept my gaze moving around the room, taking in the half-circle of bearded, swarthy men around Blome's table. The four rustlers brooded, perhaps vaguely, spiritually, listening for a knock. Bo Snecker, the reckless youth, played with a flower he had, putting the stem in his glass, then to his lips, and finally into the buttonhole of Blome's vest. Hilliard, big and gloomy, had eyes that seemed to see the hell where I expected he'd soon be. And lastly, the little dusty, scaly Pickens looked ready to leap and sting someone. The room was tense and I couldn't shake the feeling that something was about to happen.

During a lull in the conversation, Pickens spoke up, addressing someone named Jack. "Drink up and come out of it," he said. "Everyone has an off day. You've gambled long enough to know that every guy gets called out eventually. And since Foster has cashed, why do you care?"

Hilliard nodded his head in agreement, but his eyes seemed lifeless. Bo Snecker let out a laugh, which sounded no different than any other boy's laugh. I suddenly remembered that he was the one who had killed Dempsey. Sweat began to bead on my forehead. Would Foster ever come?

"Jim, the old man has cold feet and he's given them to Jack," Bo said. "It's nothing to lose your nerve once. Didn't I run like a scared jackrabbit from Foster? Watch me if he comes to life, as the old man hinted!"

"Maybe Foster wasn't in the adobe at all," someone else said. "Oh, that's a joke! I saw him in bed. I saw his shadow. I heard his shots coming from the room. Jack, you saw and heard the same as me."

"Sure, I know the Ranger's cashed," Blome replied. "It's not that. I'm just upset, boys."

"Deader than a doornail in hell!" Pickens exclaimed, lifting his glass. "Here's to Lone Star Foster's ghost! And if I saw it this minute, I'd ask it to waltz with me!"

Suddenly, the back door swung open with a violent force, and Foster burst through the doorway. He was huge, towering over everyone like a giant. Someone let out a strange, harsh cry, and Pickens dropped his glass. The room fell silent, and for a brief moment, everyone stood frozen. Foster stood with both hands out and down, leaning forward in a way I had never seen him do before. He looked like a greyhound, ready to pounce. But it wasn't just his body that was poised for action. His spirit and his nerve were there, too, like lightning about to strike. Blome remained silent, looking pale and frightened.

As soon as he realized it was the Ranger, not Foster's ghost, Blome's whole body shook as if he had been jolted out of a trance. His comrades sat motionless, but Hilliard and Pickens quickly dove under the table without rising. The others cursed and muttered, sliding and pressing back, but nobody moved to help Blome. Bo Snecker, however, stayed close to Blome, his face as white as a sheet.

Blome slowly stood up, almost instinctively, as if he didn't expect his first movement to trigger any action. Snecker sat on the edge of his chair, feet firmly planted on the floor, his eyes burning holes in his pale face. Although he was staunch and fearless, he didn't think, while Blome knew he was facing death and had no chance of surviving.

This was more than just a fight or taking stock, it was the pitiful stand of a criminal against a powerful law. Blome looked like a trapped wolf about to start a savage action, but he was equally weak and helpless. This was a lesson for the border of Pecos County; the most notorious outlaw was now a coward, unable to even draw his gun, and certain of his own doom.

However, that moment, which seemed so long, was actually very short and had to end.

Blome made a sudden movement with his shoulder and arm, causing Snecker to react quickly. Foster's actions were too fast to follow, but I saw his gun wave up and fire twice with a loud boom. Blome doubled over and fell to the floor. Snecker fired his gun as well, hitting Foster, which made me feel sick. Foster did not flinch, but Snecker's left hand went to his right arm, which had been shattered by Foster's bullet. Blood streamed everywhere, and Snecker's screams turned into curses as he went down on his knees to retrieve his gun.

Someone from the crowd warned Snecker that he was courting death, but Foster pleaded with him to surrender and promised clemency. However, Snecker continued to reach for his gun. Just as I turned my head, I saw the bartender aim a huge gun at Foster. I acted quickly and shot the bartender just in time, but he had already hit Foster. The Ranger staggered, but managed to right himself.

Without hesitation, I wheeled around to face the danger once again.

As Bo Snecker stumbled forward with his gun, a member of the crowd fired a shot, signaling chaos. People frantically ran for cover as the sound of gunfire and bullets whistling through the air filled the room. I quickly pushed Foster behind the bar, accidentally tripping over Blandy in the process.

When I stood up, I saw Foster with a gun in each hand, ready for a fight. The room was consumed by smoke, making it difficult to see. Morton and his group were also armed and engaged in the battle. The fight quickly spilled out into the street, and Foster and I ran out amidst the chaos.

As we ran, we heard gunshots coming from all directions, and it seemed like Morton's group was chasing rustlers. Suddenly, Foster collapsed in front of me, and I realized he had been shot. He was pale and covered in blood, and I thought he wouldn't make it.

However, Foster miraculously rebounded from his weakness and continued to fight with a renewed energy. He didn't even use his guns anymore, preferring to order surrender and promise protection to those who surrendered. It was as if he had no fear of bullets and was unstoppable.

Miss Barkley, who had been listening to my story, was overcome with emotion. However, she urged me to continue, and I went on to describe Foster's bravery and determination. Despite the danger, he never gave up and fought until the end.

I couldn't hold him back, and it was difficult to keep up with him. I have no idea how many times he was shot at, but it was numerous. He dragged out this and that rustler and turned them over to Morton for safekeeping. More than once, he protected a cowardly rustler from Morton's summary justice. I described Foster to Miss Barkley in detail, explaining how he appeared to me, his effect on the men, and how the rustlers were appealing to him to save them from the new vigilantes towards the end of the fight. I believed I painted a picture of the Ranger that would be etched in her memory forever. If she was a hero-worshipper, she would have had her fill.

One thing that was strange to me was the singular exultation I felt recalling Foster's look, his wonderful cold, resistless, inexplicable presence, and his unquenchable spirit that was both deadly and merciful. Other men would have killed where he saved. I remembered this magnificent spiritual something about him, strongest in the sound of his voice as he appealed to Bo Snecker not to force him to kill. Then I recounted how we left a dozen prisoners under guard and went back to the Hope So to find Blome where he had fallen. Foster's bullet had cut one of the petals of the rose Snecker had playfully put in the rustler's buttonhole. Bright and fatal target for an eye like Foster's! Bo Snecker lay clutching his gun, his face set rigidly in that last fierce expression of his savage nature. There were five other dead men on the floor, and, significant of Foster's unknown allies' work, Hilliard and Pickens were among them.

"Foster and I headed back to camp then," I concluded. "We didn't speak a word on the way out."

As soon as we arrived at camp, Foster told me to scram and leave him be. He looked like death warmed over. I obliged and wandered off a bit, but not too far. I knew what was up with him, and it wasn't no bullet wound. I was close by when he started to have his moment and fought through it.

"It's funny how some fellas can't handle the sight of blood. Never really bothered me much. I reckon I'm still human though. I sure did feel a mighty fine sense of satisfaction when I put that bullet through Blandy's thick skull. And I'll always feel that way about it. But Foster, he's a different breed altogether."

Chapter Twelve.

Foster lay in a cool, shaded glade, surrounded by towering rocks that served as our lookout. Despite his slumber, he seemed uneasy. The makeshift bandage I had fashioned from dirty rags was stained with dried blood, giving him a ghastly appearance. Green flies swarmed around him, buzzing incessantly. Even though he was a big man, he looked vulnerable and in worse shape than I had let on. When Miss Barkley caught sight of him, she gasped and clutched her chest in shock.

"Girls, keep quiet," I whispered urgently. "I don't want him to wake up suddenly and find you here. Go around the rocks and wait for me to call you."

They did as I asked, and I knelt down next to Foster, gently shaking him awake. He stirred immediately.

"Hey there," I greeted him. "You want some water?"

He blinked at me, then asked, "Water or champagne?"

I stared at him incredulously. "I've got some champagne behind the rocks," I offered.

"Weren't you listening?" he grumbled. "Water, you crazy fool!"

He looked parched and agitated, like a wild coyote in the desert.

Reaching for the canteen, I suddenly thought of how pleased Miss Barkley would be to attend to him. But I hesitated and withdrew my hand. "Hold on a minute," I said to myself before finally mustering the courage to speak up. "Vaughn, listen. Miss Barkley and Gwen are here."

He jolted so violently that I had to press him back down. "What? She's been here the whole time? Tim, you didn't double-cross me?" he asked, clearly out of his mind.

"No, Foster!" I exclaimed, trying to reassure him. "It was just a pure accident."

He seemed half-dazed, but his eyes were filled with an intense, haunting expression. "Fool! Can't you make it easier for her?" he cried out.

"This will be tough for Diane," I said, trying to ease the situation. "She needs to know things."

"Ahh," Foster breathed, sinking back. "Make it easier for her, Tim. You're a damn schemer. You've given me the double-cross, and now she's going to suffer."

"We're both in a bad situation," I replied, my words slurring slightly. "I have some crazy ideas. I'm stuck between a rock and a hard place, and I'm just about ready to give up. But still, I think you should talk to Miss Barkley, even if you can't speak clearly."

"Okay, Tim," Foster responded quickly. "But man, don't I look terrible? Covered in dirt and blood!"

"Well, if she's willing to hold your battered face in her lap, then you know she loves you," I said, trying to lift his spirits. "Don't worry too much. I'll bring the girls over."

As I walked away, I heard him groan. I went around the rocks and found the girls. "Come on," I said. "He's awake, but he's a little out of it. He gets feverish sometimes, but it won't last long."

I led Miss Barkley and Gwen back to our little campsite. Unfortunately, Foster had gotten worse in the meantime.

The foolish man had removed his bandage, causing his wound to reopen and attracting flies that he was too weak to swat away. As we approached him, his wild and captivating eyes rolled in his head. "Who's that?" he demanded. "Take it easy, old man," I responded. "I've brought the girls." Miss Barkley trembled like a leaf in the wind. "So you've come to watch me die?" Foster asked in a deep, hollow voice. Miss Barkley shot me a look of terror. "He's delirious," I explained. "Once we clean and cool his wound, he'll be fine." "Oh!" cried Miss Barkley, dropping to her knees and casting aside her gloves. She cradled Foster's head in her lap. When I saw her tears falling on his face, I felt like a villain. She leaned over him for a moment, and one of her tender hands brushed against the flow of fresh blood without flinching. "Gwen," she said, "bring the scarf from my coat. There's a veil too. Bring that. Tim, get me some water and pour it into the pan there." "Water!" whispered Foster. She gave him a drink. Gwen brought the scarf and veil, then retreated to a nearby stone and sat down. The sight of blood had made her a little pale and weak. Miss Barkley's hands trembled and her tears continued to fall, but neither hindered her tender and skillful dressing of the bullet wound. Foster said many nonsensical things. "But why did you come? Why are you being so kind when you don't love me?" "Oh, but I do love you," Miss Barkley whispered brokenly. "How do I know?" "I'm here. I'm telling you." There was a moment of silence during which she continued to bathe his head and he continued to watch her. "Diane!" he suddenly exclaimed.

"Sure, sure," he muttered, rubbing his throbbing head. "But that ain't gonna stop this pain."

"I hope it helps," she replied sympathetically.

"Kiss me then, that'll do it," he whispered. Without hesitation, she leaned in and pressed her lips to his forehead, right above the bullet wound.

"Not there," he corrected. And then, as if pulled by an invisible force, she kissed him on the lips. I couldn't look away, even though it felt like prying. That kiss was something else, something raw and beautiful. Foster looked like he was in a trance, while Diane's face was as white as snow. After she pulled away, she seemed stunned, unable to move. Foster lay there like he was dead.

I got up and went over to Gwen, putting my arm around her. "There are others," I reminded her gently.

"What's going to happen?" she asked, her voice quivering. And then she started to cry softly. I wished I could tell her everything that was going on, but I didn't even know myself. It felt like something terrible was about to happen.

Then Foster spoke again, his voice hoarse and different. I strained to hear what he was saying. "Diane, you know how hard this is for me, right?"

"Yes, I know," she replied, her voice barely above a whisper.

"You've figured out about your father, haven't you?"

"I've known for a while that you two were going to clash," she admitted. "But maybe it won't be so bad. Maybe you can bring us together."

He shushed her. "Don't talk anymore. You're too worked up right now."

"No, listen," she insisted. "I know you and my father are going to fight. But he's not what he seems, and I know that better than anyone."

"What do you mean?" he asked, his voice urgent. She looked like she was being pulled towards him, like a moth to a flame.

I feel ashamed to say it, but he has been greedy, sly, unprincipled, and dishonest," Foster confessed. Diane interrupted, trying to calm him down, but Foster continued to explain that her father was the chief of the gang that he was trying to dismantle. Diane was in disbelief and called out to her companions for help. Gwen and

Tim tried to comfort her while Foster took a moment to collect himself. When they returned to the group, Foster appeared to have regained his composure, and Diane seemed to have regained some color in her cheeks. However, when Foster mentioned that he had been dreaming, Diane blushed with embarrassment. Suddenly, Foster announced that the truth could no longer be hidden from Diane and revealed that her father was the leader of the gang of rustlers that he had been investigating. Diane was shocked, but she was also brave and demanded that Foster tell her everything.

Reuben Darling was the right-hand man of my cousin, or so I was told by Foster. Miss Barkley overheard, but didn't believe it. Foster's voice was husky as he turned away and I wished I could have lied to her. But the truth was written all over my face and she collapsed as if she had been shot. I caught her and laid her on the grass, while Gwen worked over her. Foster stood aloof, hoping she would never regain consciousness. When she did, she cried, moaned, and talked frantically. Foster staggered away, while Gwen and I tried to calm her down. We could only prevent her from hurting herself. When her emotions subsided, I left Gwen with her and went away for a while. Upon my return, Miss Barkley had regained her composure. She stood leaning against the rock where Foster had been, and was more beautiful than ever before. She asked where Foster was, but her tone and look didn't suggest the beseeching agony I had expected. I said I would find him and he came back with me. When they faced each other again, they were both different. Miss Barkley asked what Foster had to do, and he told her sternly.

The criminals outside of my own family don't concern me now. But can my father and cousin be taken without bloodshed? I want to know the absolute truth," said Miss Barkley. Foster knew that they could not be, but he could not tell her so. She then turned to me and asked for my opinion. My part in the situation grew harder. It hurt me so that it made me angry, and my anger made me cruelly frank. "No. It can't be done. Barkley and Darling will be desperately hard to approach, which'll make the chances even. So, if you must know the truth, it'll be your father and cousin to go under, or it'll be Foster or me, or any combination luck breaks or all of us!" Miss Barkley's self-control seemed to fly to the four winds. She flung herself down before Foster, against his knees, clasped her arms round him. "Good God! Miss Barkley, you mustn't do that!" implored Foster. He tried to break her hold with shaking hands, but he could not. "Listen! Listen!" she cried, and her voice made Foster, and Gwen and me also, still as the rock behind us. "Hear me! Do you think I beg you to let my father go, for his sake? No! No! I have gloried in your Ranger duty. I have loved you because of it. But some awful tragedy threatens here. Listen, Vaughn Foster. Do not you deny me, as I kneel here. I love you. I never loved any other man. But not for my love do I beseech you. "There is no help here unless you forswear your duty. Forswear it! Do not kill my father, the father of the woman who loves you. Worse and more horrible it would be to let my father kill you! It's I who make this situation unnatural, impossible. You must forswear your duty. I can live no longer if you don't. I pray you." Her voice had sunk to a whisper, and now it failed.

As she wrapped herself around him, her hair falling loose, her face turned upward, white and exhausted, her arms blindly encircling his neck, she was a vision of love, surrender, and irresistible appeal. Even without her beauty, she would have been remarkable. But with it, how could Foster have resisted? She was like a delicate, snow-white flower, suddenly shattered and ruined. In that moment, she was everything that made a woman helpless, mysterious, and sacred - everything that made her more than any other thing in life.

Until then, my eyes had been fixed on her alone. But when she tried to lift her face and he drew her up, and their two white faces met and seemed to merge into something ecstatic, awesome, and tragic, I saw Foster. He was a god, a man as beautiful as she was. They might as well have been the only two people in the world, standing alone in the heart of a desert with nothing but their love and their pain.

It was a solemn and profound moment for me. I faintly grasped how enormous it must have been for them, but all the while, the crucial matter at hand pounded in my mind. Had they forgotten, while I remembered? Perhaps it was only a moment that he held her. Perhaps it was my own agitation that conjured up such swift and whirling thoughts. But if my mind sometimes betrayed me, my eyes never did. I thought I saw Diane Barkley die in Foster's arms; I could have sworn his heart was breaking. And mine was on the brink of breaking, too.

The beauty of the couple was undeniable. He appeared strong, yet shaken, while she was tender and hopelessly appealing in her broken state. If I were in Foster's shoes, I would have forsaken everything for her. I couldn't help but feel his torture, temptation, and narrow escape. I saw the beautiful light on his face, as well as his ghastly, ashen complexion, with shaking hands that released her only to draw her back in convulsions. It was the saddest sight I had ever witnessed - the death of happiness. He had to ruin the life of the woman he loved and who loved him. I was on the verge of pulling them apart when Gwen dragged me away. Her hold on me made me feel what Miss Barkley must have felt for Foster. But when it was my own feeling, it was different. Despite my schemes and tricks to bring them together, I had an undefined fear of their embrace. However, when Gwen leaned on me and held me tight, I was glad to be led away and have a chance to regain my composure. But would I have that chance with Gwen still in the equation? Some purpose, some motive, was being born within me, and I instinctively feared Gwen because I loved her. This soft, fragile creature might be harder to move than the Ranger, but could she sense my yet-to-be-formed motive?

Suddenly, a wave of calm washed over me and I was able to hide my true feelings. "What's wrong with you, Tim?" Gwen asked urgently. "Can't we leave this awful place and focus on our own happiness?" "I suppose we should," I replied, struggling against her alluring charm. I knew I had to keep my mouth shut or else I would reveal my true feelings. "You look different, Tim. I don't want you to kiss me with those closed lips. Smile and kiss me," she pleaded. "You're so cold and distant. You're giving me chills!" "I'm shaken up, dear. Let me be alone to think things through," I said, trying to break free from her embrace. But she held on tighter, sensing my discomfort and the turmoil inside me. "Women are so intuitive," I thought to myself. I knew I had to get away quickly before I lost control. Gwen's loving gaze met mine as her hands slid down my shoulders, behind my neck, and locked there like steel bands. This was my test. Would it be as difficult as Foster's had been? I prepared myself for the worst and swore that I would remain strong no matter what.

Gwen let out a cry that pierced my heart, and then she was pressed up against me. Her chest was heaving against mine, and her eyes, now dark as night, were searching my soul. She saw more than I knew, and with her tight embrace, she confirmed my fears. Then she kissed me, with a passion that had nothing to do with girlhood or coquetry. It was a woman's passion to blind and tame. The intensity of her kisses made me feel like a tiger, and it was that tiger that prevented me from succumbing to her allure.

"I'm your promised wife, Tim!" she whispered desperately. "You said soon. I want it to be tomorrow!"

All the subtlety, intelligence, cunning, charm, and love that made up a woman's power were in her plea. It was torture to hear, and I felt like I was being pulled in two different directions. If the calamity had been mine alone, I might have laughed it off and taken Gwen at her word. But I had a responsibility to Foster.

I told her in short, husky sentences what depended on Foster: that I loved the Ranger Service, but loved him more; that his character and life embodied the Service I loved; that I had ruined him, and now I would take his place and do his work, even if it meant risking my life.

"It's great of you, dearest," she cried. "But the cost! If you kill one of my kin, I'll I'll shrink from you! If you're killed Oh, the thought is dreadful! You've done your share. Let Foster or another Ranger finish it. I swear I'm not pleading for my uncle or my cousin, for their sakes. If they're vile, let them suffer."

"Gwen, it's all about you!" I exclaimed. "My dreams were shattered when I realized that I won't be able to show you my beautiful home with its oranges, mossy trees, and mocking-birds. It's a pity that you won't be able to come and see it now."

"But Tim, there's still a chance, a slight chance that I can do the job without...," Gwen trailed off.

Before she could finish her sentence, she let go of me and I quickly drew her towards the stone. I cursed the day I ever met Neal and got involved in the service. Gwen's arch prettiness and sweet charm were nowhere to be found. She looked like she was suffering from a desperate physical injury. Her final breakdown showed that I was lost to her, no matter what.

As she sank on the stone, I had my supreme wrench, leaving me numb, hard, and in a cold sweat. "Don't betray me! I'll forestall him! He's planned nothing for today," I whispered hoarsely. "Gwen, you are the dearest, gamest little girl in the world! Remember that I loved you, even if I couldn't prove it your way. It's all for his sake. I'm to blame for their love. Someday, my act will look different to you. Goodbye!"

Chapter Thirteen.

I sprinted down the rugged slope with a fervor that felt like I was possessed by demons. The wind roared in my ears, but there was another sound mixed in that I couldn't identify. When I reached a level surface, I kept running, but it felt like something was pulling me back. I gradually slowed to a walk, bewildered by this new sensation that was unlike anything I had ever experienced. It was as if one side of my mind was fixed on a particular goal, while the other was a jumbled mess of thoughts and sensations. I couldn't calm down, no matter how hard I tried.

Eventually, I found myself hurrying again, almost without realizing it. I kept glancing over my shoulder, half-expecting to see someone chasing me. The action of running seemed to ease the burden of my oppressive state, so I continued on, picking up speed as I went.

As I journeyed further, the task at hand became increasingly difficult. By continuing on this path, I would be forsaking love, happiness, and the potential for success in life. I was making this choice, but it wasn't one I had made absolutely. I knew I needed to be completely certain before proceeding. A clear warning thought came to me, telling me that the work I was pursuing so fervently could not be accomplished with the mindset I currently had. I clung to this thought. Multiple times I slowed my pace, and even stopped altogether, but eventually I trudged on.

Finally, as I crested a small hill, I saw Linrock laid out before me, vibrant and lush. It wasn't far away, and this sight caused me to come to a definitive halt. There were mesquites on the ridge, and I sought refuge in their shade. It was noon, and the sun beat down mercilessly with no breeze to offer relief. It was here that I had to face my inner turmoil. I had lived a life full of adventure, but never had I struggled so hard to comprehend myself and my situation. I was not the same man I had once been, and I couldn't seem to revert back to that person.

The reason for this was clear. It was Gwen Langdon, the vivacious and mischievous girl who had entranced me. She had transformed over the weeks, still possessing her old charms while acquiring new traits that made her the perfect woman to make my life beautiful. She had become a woman of loyalty, passion, and love. Temptation threatened to overtake me. She had promised to be my wife in just twenty-four hours. The thought of having her as mine was tantalizing. She was the only woman I had ever truly desired, the only one who had brought out the best in me.

As I rode the stagecoach back to Austin, I couldn't help but think about her home. The place where oranges grew and the trees were decorated with gray moss and the mockingbirds sang beautiful melodies. I imagined myself riding through the cotton, rice, and cane fields, arriving at the grand mansion where long-eared hounds would welcome me with their baying and a lovely woman would greet me with a happy smile. I could picture the children too, Gwen as their mother and myself as their father. It was the kind of life I had always yearned for as a lonely Ranger.

These thoughts stirred something deep within me, something new and strange that I couldn't quite explain. The temptation of this all-satisfying prospect made me feel physically weak and my spirit faint and low. But why had I turned my back on it? Was it worth it to arrest and jail a few rustlers or to face Barkley and show him my shield and reach for my gun? Was it worth it to kill Darling or to save the people of Linrock from greed, raids, and murder? Was it worth it to please and aid Neal, my old captain of the Rangers, or to save the Service to the State? No, a thousand times no. It was all for Foster, the wonderful man that I had undone by throwing Diane Barkley into his arms. That was my great error.

This Ranger was the envy and admiration of his peers. He was a remarkable specimen - disciplined, principled, and dedicated to the Service. He embodied the spirit of Texas, which stood steadfast against disorder and crime. To us, he was the epitome of what it meant to be a Ranger.

Despite his unwavering commitment to the law, he was not immune to the charms of a woman. However, he remained resolute in his duties, and no amount of passion could sway him. I, too, had fallen for him, but I knew that my love was futile.

As we worked on the Linrock case, it became clear that his career was on the line. If he failed, he would be ruined, and the Service would suffer. It was then that I realized that I had to save him -

not for love, but for duty. I knew that I would have to take down Barkley or Darling, even if it meant being ostracized by Gwen Langdon.

I had no illusions about our relationship. I knew that I had to let him go, and in doing so, I felt a coldness in my soul. But I was willing to make that sacrifice for the greater good.

After a period of regret, pain, and darkness, I emerged bitter and callous, ready for a difficult and deadly mission. I forgot about Miss Barkley, and even Gwen became a distant memory. Instead, my mind was consumed by thoughts of Snecker, Barkley, and Darling - all with their own menacing possibilities. The thrill of the man-hunt returned, more intense than ever before.

When I arrived in Linrock around one o'clock, the streets were deserted. I headed straight to the hall where Morton and Zimmer were keeping watch over the prisoners. They seemed restless and anxious, and I soon learned that only half of the original number of prisoners remained. Morton claimed they had escaped, but I wasn't sure whether to believe him.

I tried to ask more questions, but Morton and Zimmer were eager to speak their minds. They demanded to know where Foster was, and I explained that he was out of town and unable to act. They were pleased to hear this, as they had grown tired of waiting. The gang had already split, and if they acted quickly, they could prevent them from reuniting.

Old man Snecker had shown up that day, and was drawing the gang back together. He was furious after Bo's death, and would be a dangerous opponent if he became fully involved. He was currently at the Hope So with a dozen other gang members, and was the only known leader left.

"We need to get him," I said, looking around the group of men. "If we catch him, we can finally break the rustler gang for good."

"He sent word down here demanding we release our prisoners, or there'll be a damn bloody fight," one of the men reported. "We haven't given our answer yet. We were hoping Foster would show up, but now we're glad you're back."

"I'll take care of the answer," I replied quickly. "But first, do you know if Barkley and Darling are at the ranch?"

"They were there an hour ago," the man confirmed. "Zimmer saw Dick."

"Good. Do you have any horses we can use?" I asked.

"Sure. The ones outside belong to us," he said.

"Great. I need you to take a man with you and ride around the back roads up to Barkley's house. Wait under the trees until you hear me shoot or yell, then come fast," I instructed.

The man's face went pale. "So that's where the scent leads," he muttered. "We always wondered, half-believed, but no one had any nerve to say anything."

"Can I count on you?" I asked.

"Absolutely," he replied, his voice shaking.

"Good. That's all. Come out and get me a horse," I said, heading towards the door.

As I mounted my horse and rode towards the Hope So, I formulated my plan for dealing with Snecker. I needed to be bold and go straight into the saloon. I'd ask for the rustler, pretending to have a reply from Morton. Then, I'd whisper a message supposedly from Barkley and see if Snecker took the bait. If he did, I could surprise him and kill him, then run for my horse.

The plan seemed clever to me, but I couldn't help but worry about the risks. The rustlers may have seen my involvement in Foster's defense the other day, but that was a risk I was willing to take. There were always risks to face.

I arrived at the Hope So saloon, knowing that I had been spotted. Despite feeling cold, I was also exhilarated. Walking into the saloon, I saw that it was full of men, with some behind the bar. Blandy's place had not been filled. As I entered, every face turned towards me, scowling and dark. I needed my nerve to speak up, calling out for Snecker. However, nobody moved. I scanned the crowd but did not see Snecker. "I'm in a hurry," I said. "Bill ain't here," replied a man at the table closest to me. "Are you coming from Morton?" "No, but I'm not yelling this message," I retorted. The rustler got up and strode towards me. "Word from Barkley!" I whispered, and he stared at me. "I'm in his confidence. He's got to see Bill at once. Barkley sends word he's quit, he's done, he's through. The jig is up, and he means to hit the road out of Linrock." "Bill'll kill him surer'n hell," muttered the rustler. "But we all said it'd come to that. And what'd Darling say?" "Darling!

Why, he's dead. Didn't you hear? Reckon Barkley shot him." The rustler cursed and clenched his fist. "When did Darling get it?" "A little while ago. I don't know how long. Anyway, I saw him lying dead on the porch. And say, pard, I've got to go. Send Bill up quick as he comes. Tell him Barkley wants to turn over all his stock and then light out." I backed towards the door, and the rustler remained in a scowling amazement. I had fooled him, but I needed Snecker to arrive soon.

I mounted my horse and leisurely trotted up the street. Linrock was a ghost town, with stores barricaded and business at a standstill. However, I did see a few people, a buckboard, and some cattle wandering around. When I reached the edge of town, I turned aside for a moment to take a look at the ruins of Foster's adobe house. It was nothing but rubble, completely destroyed. Foster had left nothing behind that could have been of any use to him. I continued on my way up to the ranch, my mind eager for distractions to escape the grim reality of the situation.

As I was about halfway across the flat, I heard the rapid clatter of hoofs on the hard road. I turned to see who it was, expecting to see Morton and his man, but it was only one man on a fine bay horse. It was Snecker, and he was in a hurry. I was completely astonished to see him, and I quickly got on my guard. I booted my horse so hard that he reared up, and I pulled out my gun, holding it concealed under my sombrero. This rustler had been giving me trouble, and here he was, galloping towards me alone. I felt a rush of exultation, but then my temper settled and I waited in breathless suspense.

As I sat atop my horse, Snecker rode up beside me and came to a sudden stop. I couldn't help but feel fortunate - I always seemed to have luck on my side during these dangerous dealings. Snecker appeared to be seething with anger, like a volcano ready to erupt. His wide-brimmed hat and thick beard concealed most of his face, except for his fiery eyes that burned with intensity. Both he and his lieutenant had been thrown off balance by the strange message supposedly from Barkley. It was Barkley's name that had lured and fooled these men.

"Hey! You're the guy who left a message for someone at the Hope So?" Snecker barked at me.

"Yes," I replied calmly, patting my horse's neck with my left hand to keep him still. "Barkley wants me bad, huh?"

"I reckon there's only one man who wants you more," Snecker retorted.

I met his piercing gaze with a steady stare. This was a rustler who wouldn't be fooled for long. I remained calm and collected, waiting with certainty.

"You that cowboy, Tim?" he asked.

"I was and I'm not," I replied with a significant tone.

Snecker's violent outburst was sudden and explosive. "What the hell!" he exclaimed. "Bill, you're easy."

"Who are you?" he demanded hoarsely, his hand already reaching for his gun.

I watched Snecker like a hawk, waiting for the right moment to strike. "United States deputy marshal. Bill, you're under arrest!" I declared.

In a fit of rage, he drew his gun, but I was quicker. I shot through my hat and hit Snecker's horse, causing it to buck and throw him off. His foot got caught in the stirrup, and the panicked horse dragged him along for a few jumps before his foot slipped loose. Snecker lay motionless in the road, and I knew my bullet had hit its mark.

As I rode into Barkley's courtyard and dismounted, I could hear loud and angry voices coming from inside.

Barkley and Darling were having another argument. Luckily, fate was on my side. Though I had no plan, my mind raced with a hundred different ideas. The yelling stopped abruptly, and both men emerged onto the porch. I immediately put on my best impression of an impudent, drunken cowboy. "It's just Tim and he's drunk," Reuben Darling sneered. "I heard horses trotting off," Barkley said. "Maybe the girls are coming. I bet I teach them not to run off again. Hello, Tim." Barkley seemed friendly enough, despite his haggard appearance. He was in his shirt sleeves, with a gun in his hand that he placed on a table nearby. I rode up to the porch and greeted them briefly, playing the part of a clumsy cowboy dismounting from his horse. As soon as I stood up straight, I knew I had them. It was the moment I had been waiting for, and I was ready. I acted and looked exactly like the cowboy I was pretending to be, even though I was overwhelmed by intense emotions: passion, suspense, and nausea. All I wanted was to get Barkley and Darling together, or failing that, to position myself so I had a chance. I kept my eyes on Barkley's gun and the table, knowing that two of the objects could move at any moment. "What do you want here?" Darling demanded. He was red-faced and sweaty from drinking, but sober enough to know what was going on. "Me? Say, Darling, I ain't fired yet," I replied, my resentment rising. "Well, you're fired now," he replied insolently.

"Who do you think you are, firing me?" I strolled up to the porch with a cigarette in my hand and a match in the other. As I lit my cigarette, a voice replied, "I do," and I turned to face Darling. It was clear to me that Barkley was hoping for a confrontation between us. "Ha! You fired me once before and it didn't stick, Darling. You're not as tough as you think."

Darling was clearly distracted, lost in his own thoughts. It was obvious that strong forces were at work. Both men were on edge, and I could tell that Darling was close to breaking. Barkley laughed mockingly at my words, which only served to anger Darling more. He stopped pacing and turned his fiery gaze towards me. "Barkley, I won't tolerate this man's impudence."

"Come on, Darling, don't be like that," I said. "Barkley knows I'm a good guy, and I've got you figured out, too."

"You better leave, Tim," warned Barkley. "We're busy with deals today, and we're expecting visitors."

"Sure, I don't want to stick around where I'm not wanted," I replied, taking a drag from my cigarette. I didn't move from my spot, though. Barkley sat in a chair near the door, with his gun on the table between him and Darling. It was clear that he didn't want any trouble.

"Why did you come here anyway?" Barkley asked me suddenly.

"Well, I had some news to share," I said.

"Then get on with it," he replied.

"Look, Mr. Barkley, I'm a sensitive guy. I don't want to hurt anyone's feelings."

"If I were to tell Mr. Darling this news, he'd go crazy," I said sarcastically. Darling was angry, but also curious. Barkley probably thought I was drunk, and if I hadn't rubbed Darling the wrong way, he wouldn't have even let me talk. "What's the news?" asked Darling. "You don't have to worry about hurting my feelings." "I'm not so sure about that," I drawled. "It's about the girl you like and the ranger you don't like." Barkley jumped up. "Tim, did Diane go out to meet Foster?" he asked angrily. "Yes, she did," I replied. Darling looked like he was about to choke. Both men were getting excited, moving around and waking up. I waited patiently, keeping my emotions in check. "How do you know she met Foster?" demanded Barkley. "I was there. I met Gwen at the same time," I said. "But why would my daughter meet this Ranger?" asked Barkley. "She's in love with him and he's in love with her," I stated plainly. The statement hit them hard. I enjoyed seeing Darling's reaction, but I felt bad for Barkley. He still had his pride, and now he was wondering if his daughter would side against him. He seemed to age right before my eyes. Darling found his voice and cursed Diane, the Ranger, Barkley, and me. "You selfish fool!" Barkley cried in bitter scorn. "All you care about is yourself and losing the girl. Think about me, my home, my life!" Then it seemed to dawn on Barkley that somehow, through his daughter, he and his cousin would be betrayed.

Although I couldn't be sure, it seemed to me that jealousy was the main emotion Darling was feeling. Barkley shoved me off the porch, demanding that I leave. Without checking to see if I would return, he turned to face Darling. They stood close to each other, with Barkley on the other side of the table where the gun sat. This was my chance. I knew I had the upper hand in this game, and it felt like a burst of energy exploded in my brain and spread throughout my body.

"You'll never have her," Barkley exclaimed, his voice full of hatred and menace. "I'd rather see her be Ranger Foster's wife than yours, so help me God!"

Darling was shocked by this statement, and Barkley took advantage of his confusion. "You made me who I am, Darling," Barkley continued. "I supported you, protected you, and even joined forces with you. But now, I'm done. I quit you."

Their faces were unmoving, and their passion was like stones. I knew I had to take control of the situation. "Gentlemen," I called out in a clear, authoritative voice, "you're both finished!"

They turned to face me, and I had my gun pointed at them. "Don't move a muscle! Not a finger!" I warned them. Barkley understood the danger he was in, but Darling was too consumed by his anger to comprehend the situation. I raised my left hand to show them my shield, which was gleaming in the sunlight. "I am a United States deputy marshal in the service of Ranger Foster!"

Darling howled like a wild animal and made a reckless attempt to grab his gun. But my shot was quick and precise, cutting short his life and his foolishness.

Before Darling even stumbled, before he let go of the gun, Barkley jumped behind him, wrapped his left arm around him, and snatched the gun from both of his hands and put it away in a flash. I fired at Barkley, then again, then a third time. All of my bullets went into the nodding Darling's lifted body. Barkley had shielded himself with the corpse. I saw red flashes, puffs of smoke, and heard quick reports. Something stung my left arm. Then I was hit by a light yet impactful blow that knocked me down. The hot lead followed the blow. My heart felt like it was exploding, yet my mind was clear and quick. I got up, leaned on a post by my shoulder, and heard Barkley work the action of Darling's gun. I heard the hammer click and fall upon empty shells. He had used up all of Darling's gun's loads. I heard him curse, defeated. I waited, now cool and confident, for him to reveal himself from behind his bolster. He tried to lift the dead man and move him closer to the table where the gun was, but he found the task too risky. He bent over, peering at me under Darling's arm. Barkley's eyes were those of a man who intended to kill me. There was no mistaking the strange and terrible light in eyes like those. I had more than one chance to aim at them, at the top of Barkley's head, or at a strip of his side. But I had only two shells left, and I wanted to be sure. Suddenly, I remembered Morton and his man. Then I let out a hoarse, strange, yet far-reaching cry. It was answered by a shout. Barkley heard it, and it brought out all that was inside him. He threw Darling's body aside.

Before Barkley could even jump for his gun, I aimed mine at him and warned him not to move. I had the upper hand and he knew it. With two shots left, I could easily take him out. But, I gave him one chance to surrender. I pleaded with him to think of his daughter and offered him a deal. I had all the evidence against him and he was cornered. But, if he surrendered, I would spare his life and let him go back to his old country. It was for his daughter's sake.

Barkley stood there, calculating his chances. He was a brave man and I respected him for it. I could see him measuring the distance to his gun, determined to make a move. I knew I had to act fast before it was too late.

I called out to him again, urging him to surrender. I told him that I had killed his accomplices and that he was alone. I could see Morton and his men coming to my aid. I gave Barkley an ultimatum - surrender or face death.

Barkley asked what would happen if he refused. I told him that I would kill him right then and there. He knew I was serious. I urged him to be a man and surrender for his daughter's sake.

Finally, Barkley gave in. He walked to the chair and sat down, just as Morton and his men arrived. I ordered them to put away their guns and told them that the game was up. Barkley was my prisoner and I gave him my word that he would be protected.

Your job is to draft the necessary documents with him. He's willing to split his entire estate - every inch of land, every livestock - as per your and Zimmer's instructions. He's relinquishing everything. Once the process is complete, he'll be allowed to leave the country, and he must never come back.

Chapter Fourteen.

Barkley stared at the bloody stain on my chest, causing my thoughts to race. Morton rushed up the stairs, his face etched with concern. When he saw me, he stopped in his tracks and opened his arms wide. "The girls are coming!" Barkley exclaimed suddenly. "Morton, help me get Darling inside. They can't see him." I faced the porch, watching as Miss Barkley and Gwen approached, clearly worried. Foster was probably still at camp. I wondered what they would say and do when they arrived. Suddenly, Barkley and Johnson came to carry me inside. They laid me on the couch in the parlor where the girls used to spend time. "Tim, you're in bad shape," said Barkley, leaning over me and placing his hands on my chest. The room was filled with sunlight, but it seemed to be fading. "I reckon I am," I replied. "I'm sorry. If only you had told me sooner! Darling, damn him! He's always been a problem for me!" "But the last time, Barkley." "Yes, and I almost drove you to kill me too. Tim, you talked me out of it. For Diane's sake! She'll be here any minute. This will be harder than facing a gun." "It's hard now. But it'll be okay." "Tim, can you do me a favor?" he asked, looking embarrassed. "Of course." "Let Diane and Gwen think Darling shot you. He's dead now. It doesn't matter.

And you're hurt. The girls care about you. If you don't make it, the old side of my life will return. It's been creeping back."

"It'll be here any minute now, just as she enters this room. And damn, I'd switch places with you if I could," Barkley said.

"I'm glad you said that, Barkley," I replied. "Darling got me, but it's our little secret. I had my reasons, not that it matters much now."

The light was fading, and I struggled to talk. I felt numb, like I was encased in ice, with occasional prickles of sensation and rushing sounds in my ears. But my mind was clear. There wasn't much to be done. Morton came in, looked at me, and left. I heard the girls' light footsteps on the porch and murmuring voices.

"Where did I get hit?" I whispered.

"Three places. Arm, shoulder, and a bad one in the chest. It hit your lung, I'm afraid. But if you leave now, you might have a chance," Barkley replied.

"Sure, I've got a chance."

"Tim, I'll tell the girls, do what I can for you, then take care of Morton and get out of here," Barkley said.

Just then, Diane and Gwen entered the room. I heard two low cries, so different in tone, and saw two dim white faces. Gwen rushed to my side and dropped to her knees. Both of her hands went to my face, then to my chest. She lifted them, shaking. They were red. White and silent, she stared from them to me. But some woman's intuition kept her from fainting.

"Papa!" Diane cried, wringing her hands.

"Don't lose your nerve," Barkley replied. "Both of you will need it. Tim is badly hurt. There's little hope for him."

Gwen moaned and dropped her face against me, holding me tightly. I tried to reach out and touch her, but I couldn't move. I felt her hair against my face. Diane let out a low, heartbreaking cry, which Barkley and I understood.

"Let me tell you what happened quickly," Barkley said hoarsely. "There was a fight. Tim killed Snecker and Darling. They resisted arrest. If it was Darling, it was his gun that took Tim down."

Tim released me. He didn't just let me go, he saved me, Diane. I have to divide my property and return what I've stolen. I have to leave Texas immediately and never come back. If you ever want to come home, you'll find me in old Louisiana." As she stood there, realizing she was saved, her eyes shifted from her father to me. My own eyes clouded, and I thought if I were dying then, it was not in vain. "Send for Foster," I whispered. They worked over me silently and quickly. I was sensitive to touch and sound, but I couldn't see anything. Eventually, everything was quiet, and I drifted into a black void. Suddenly, heavy footsteps jarred into the blackness and I opened my eyes to see Gwen's haggard face, Miss Barkley flying to the door, and the stalwart Ranger entering. Life rushed back into me with agonizing pain in every nerve. I saw him start and heard him cry, but I couldn't speak. He bent over me, and I tried to smile. He stood there silently, his hand on me while Diane Barkley told him what had happened. She finished the story with her head on his shoulder, tears falling for me. For the first time, I saw him stunned. When he recovered, he didn't think of Diane or the end of Barkley's power. He turned to me.

"There's no way this bullet hole can take down a Ranger like me!" the man exclaimed with a powerful voice. "Don't lose hope just yet!" I couldn't respond, but I managed to crack a smile. Unlike the faces of Gwen and Diane, his was free of pain and despair. He fought death with the same vigor he fought evil, and his presence alone lifted the spirits of the girls. Diane began to believe in a positive outcome, while Gwen's sorrow dissipated. The room was transformed by his aura, a force as big, strong, and virile as himself. His mere presence made me want to live, and suddenly, I felt alive. It was like a jolt of electricity running through me, reawakening every deadened nerve. I went from being numb to feeling pain, and that pain soon turned into a fever. My mind drifted in and out of consciousness, with Gwen's ghostly figure appearing and disappearing, and Diane taking care of me during my lucid moments. But the Ranger was always there, sometimes appearing in my dreams as a protector, warding off dark and ominous figures. The fever eventually broke, and as I sipped on my first nourishing drink, I found my voice. "Hey there, old man," I whispered to Foster. "Can't believe you'd double-cross me like that!" His good-natured rebuke let me know that death was the furthest thing from his mind when it came to me.

He knew what he was doing. He even laughed at me. I had to do it." Gwen sat down on the bed and took my hand. "Tim, you must forget it. It was inevitable. You were defending yourself. You had to do it. Don't let it ruin your life." I looked at her, and in that moment, all my brooding and despair vanished. Her words were like a balm to my soul, and I felt a renewed sense of hope and purpose. I realized then that I had been foolish to let my mind dwell on negative thoughts and that I needed to focus on healing and moving forward. Gwen's presence was like a ray of sunshine in my dark world, and I knew that with her by my side, I could overcome anything.

"I ain't got no excuse," I said.

"Hush now, tell me. If you had confronted them and drew on them, then you had a chance to kill my uncle?" Diane asked.

"Yes, I could have done it easily," I replied.

"Why didn't you then?" she asked.

"It was for Diane's sake. I'm afraid I didn't think of you. I had put you out of my mind," I explained.

"Well, if a man can be noble at the same time he's terrible, you've been, Tim. I don't know how I feel. I'm sick and I can't think. I see, though, what you saved Diane and Foster. Why, she's touching happiness again, fearfully, yet really. Think of that! God only knows what you did for Foster. If I judged it by his suffering as you lay there about to die, it would be beyond words to tell. But, Tim, you're pale and shaky now. Hush! No more talk!" Diane said.

I watched Diane closely, wondering if she would shrink away from me. She was gentle as she smoothed my pillow and moved my head, but there was a dark abstraction hanging over her that was foreign to her nature. It was a moment where my sensitivities were on high alert. However, I saw and felt and knew that she did not shrink from me. My thoughts and feelings escaped me for a while, and I dozed off. When I woke up, Foster and Diane had just come in. As Foster bent over me, I looked up into his keen gray eyes, and there was no mask on my own as I looked up to him.

"Son, the thing that was needed was a change of nurses," he said gently. "I intend to make up some sleep now and leave you in better care."

From that hour, I improved. I slept, I lay quietly awake, I ate nourishing food. I listened and watched, and all the time I gained.

I didn't say much, and even though I tried to lighten the mood when Foster was around, I wasn't very successful. Time passed, and Gwen was almost always with me, but never alone. She wasn't as cheerful as she used to be, and it broke my heart. I prayed for her to recover, to hear the old joy back in her voice. But Gwen had been through a traumatic experience that left a deep scar on her soul, almost as dangerous as the wound I had received. I still held onto hope, though. I had seen other women recover from similar situations and become their old selves again. However, as I observed her more closely, I realized that time alone wouldn't be enough for Gwen to heal. She was afraid of everything, always on edge, and terrified of the dark. It was then that I realized one of the reasons for her strange behavior. The house where I had killed one of her relatives would always haunt her. She had told me that she was a Southerner and that blood was thicker than water. It was clear that she couldn't stay in that house any longer.

I sat up in bed, startling all my kind nurses. "Foster, I won't recover in this house. I need to go home. When can we leave?" They tried to persuade me to stay and scolded me for insisting on leaving. But when they saw the determination in my eyes, they finally agreed to plan for our departure in a few days, provided that I improved. We would ride out of Pecos County together, back along the stage trail to civilization. The look in Gwen's eyes confirmed my decision. I could have left that very day and endured any pain or discomfort.

It was strange to witness the response of Foster and Diane to my idea, to the promise of what lay beyond the wild and barren hills. Foster recounted to me that very day about the headlong flight of every lawless character out of Linrock, the very hour that Snecker, Darling, and Barkley were known to have fallen. Foster expressed deep feeling, almost mortification, that the credit of that final coup had gone to him instead of me. His denial and explanation had been only a few soundless words in the face of a grateful and clamorous populace that tried to reward him, to make him the mayor of Linrock.

Barkley had made restitution in every case where he had personally gained at the loss of a farmer or rancher, and the accumulation of years went far toward returning to Linrock what it had lost in a material way. When he boarded the stage for Sanderson to leave Texas forever, he had been a poor man.

Not long afterward, I heard Foster talking to Miss Barkley, in a deep and agitated voice. "You must rise above this. When I come upon you alone, I see the shadow, the pain in your face. How wonderfully this thing has turned out when it might have ruined you! I expected it to ruin you. Who, but that wild boy in there, could have saved us all? Diane, you have had cause for sorrow. But your father is alive and will live it down. Perhaps, back there in Louisiana, the dishonor will never be known. Pecos County is far from your old home. And even in San Antonio and Austin, a man's evil repute means little.

"Then the line between a rustler and a rancher is hard to draw in these wild border days. Rustling is stealing cattle, and I once heard a well-known rancher say that all rich cattlemen had done a little stealing. Your father drifted out here, and like a good many others, he succeeded."

Judging him by the laws and morals of a civilized country might not be worth the effort. He somehow ended up with the wrong crowd, and it's possible that an honest deal tied his hands and led him astray. The matter of land, water, and a few head of stock had to be decided outside the court, and he probably didn't realize where he was heading. However, one thing led to another, and he found himself in the midst of crooked dealings. To protect himself, he bound men to him, and that's how the gang developed. Many powerful gangs have developed that way out here. He couldn't control them, and he became involved with them. Eventually, their dealings became deliberately dishonest, and that meant that blood would be spilled sooner or later. He became the leader because he was the strongest, but he could have been worse.

When he stopped talking, I felt the same impulse that must have motivated Foster to show Barkley in a better light than he was painted, to give him the benefit of the doubt, and to judge him justly in the eyes of Rangers who knew what wild border life was like. "Foster, bring Diane in!" I called. "I have something to tell her." They came quickly, probably concerned about my tone. "I've been hoping for a chance to tell you something, Miss Barkley. That day I came here, your father was quarreling with Darling. I had heard them do that before. He hated Darling. The reason came out just before we had the fight. It was my plan to surprise them. I did. I told them you went out to meet Foster, that you two were in love with each other. Darling grew wild. He swore no one would ever have you. Then Barkley said he'd rather have you as Foster's wife than Darling's. I'll never forget that scene."

Before you arrived in Linrock, there was a lot of history behind it all. Your father mentioned that he had supported Darling, but the deal had ruined him and turned him into a rustler. He claimed that he was finished with it all. I understand everything now, and I want to clarify things for you, Miss Barkley. It was actually Darling who ruined your father. He was the one who was rustling and he caused the gang to form. However, Darling didn't have the intelligence or ability to lead the gang, so your father became the leader because they were related by blood. Your father was never a true criminal at heart. "I respected him because he proved himself to be a man in the end. He faced me to be shot, but I couldn't do it." Foster mentioned that you have a reason to be sad, but you need to move on and not dwell on it. In my opinion, you haven't been disgraced or dishonored. However, the important thing is whether or not a woman like you, who values honor, has a real and lasting reason to feel ashamed. Foster and I both agree that you don't. Then, Miss Barkley came and sat beside me with tears in her eyes and

Gwen entered the room to see her cousin kissing me gratefully with sisterly affection. It was a woman's kiss, given purely out of gratitude. Gwen couldn't understand it; it was too sudden and unexpected. Despite the dark stain between us, I could tell from the way her face turned red that she still loved me.

Chapter Fifteen.

Four mornings after, we found ourselves on board the stagecoach, making our way down the main street, departing from Linrock. The entire town had gathered to say their goodbyes.

The raucous cheering and fervor of the crowd was getting on my nerves. I just couldn't see things from their perspective. I was feeling pretty morose and the whole world seemed to hinge on one thing. Morton was stubborn about sending an escort with us to Del Rio. The escort was made up of six cowboys, mounted and carrying light packs, and they rode ahead of the stage. Luckily, we had the stagecoach all to ourselves. A comfortable bed had been fashioned for me by laying boards across the seats and furnishing it with blankets and pillows. My three companions managed to squeeze in as well, but Foster made it clear that he would be spending most of the ride outside. Miss Barkley didn't seem too thrilled about the prospect of being stuck inside with me either. It meant that I would be alone with Gwen. The thought excited and saddened me at the same time. How different this ride was from our first one, which had been full of adventure and promise!

"It's over!" exclaimed Foster, sounding relieved. "It's done! I'm glad for their sakes and ours. We're finally out of town."

I was too preoccupied to notice the shouts and cheers of the crowd. But I did notice a subtle change in Gwen Langdon's expression. We hadn't even traveled a mile before the tension in her face melted away, and her downcast eyelids lifted. I could see a lighter spirit in her, without a doubt. That's when I allowed myself to relax. I had been so tense, trying to hold myself together for this journey. I lay back with my eyes closed, feeling exhausted, in more pain than I wanted to admit. And I thought and thought. Miss Barkley had said to me: "Tim, it'll all work out. I can tell you something now that you never knew. Gwen had a soft spot for our cousin, Reuben Darling, for years. She hadn't seen him since she was a child, but she remembered him."

Gwen Langdon was left without any family after her brother Arthur was killed in the Rebellion. Reuben and I were her closest relatives, and she had been looking forward to meeting Reuben out West. However, Reuben disappointed her by being a heavy drinker, which she hated. Despite this, she could never fully hate him because he reminded her of Arthur. When Reuben was killed, Gwen was shocked and haunted by it. I stayed with her on those nights, and Vaughn and I have since been studying and talking about her. We believe she is gradually recovering, but she still loves me just as she loved Arthur. I was told to not brood and be patient, but what did I know about women? I couldn't be sure if I had killed Gwen's love for me or if she still loved me but couldn't break down the barrier between us.

Our journey began with physical distress, but I eventually grew accustomed to the roll of the stagecoach. We stopped in the small town of Barkley, where Foster got letters from reliable ranchers to verify his Ranger report for Captain Neal.

To ensure Governor Smith had all the necessary evidence, Foster took the precaution of leaving a blank line in his report, omitting the name of the mysterious leader of the Pecos gang. This news was shared as Foster returned to us and entered the stage, with a gray flame in his eyes. He spoke of his report, claiming it to be the longest and best he had ever turned in, but he had no intention of allowing Tim to read it due to his peevishness towards Foster's desire to put his part on record.

Foster went on to explain that many had suspected, but few had known the identity of the supposed leader, and he had taken measures to ensure their silence. With the death of Jack Blome and his associates, Linrock was now free and safe, with its future in the hands of determined and capable men.

We all sat in silence, with Diane's face showing a mix of sorrow and joy. It was clear she was overwhelmed by the news. After a moment, I dared to say that Vaughn Foster, Lone Star Ranger, had seen his last service. He confirmed this with emotion.

Gwen, who had been quiet until now, turned to us with a strange look and said, "In that case, then, if I am not mistaken, there were two Lone Star Rangers, and both have seen their last service!" Her lips trembled, and it was impossible to tell if she was about to laugh or cry. This was the first hint of her old combative spirit or archness, which stirred a wave of feeling in me that was too much to handle in my weakened condition.

My head was spinning, and my body was wracked with sudden shooting pains. I closed my eyes tightly, trying to focus on the happiness I felt despite the suffering. The sound of something beating echoed in my ears, pulsing with the same rapid rhythm as my own blood. Not too late! Not too late!

From that moment on, the ride was different. I improved with each passing moment, leaving Sanderson, the long gray barren between Sanderson and the Rio Grande, and Del Rio behind us. After two days in Del Rio, where I was able to sit up, we headed towards the eastward trail to Uvalde. We were the only passengers on the stagecoach from Del Rio to Uvalde, which was probably arranged by Foster, who had become an individual with whom traveling under the curious gaze of strangers would have been embarrassing. He was most desperately in love with Diane, who had renewed her bloom and gained what she had lost during the long, tedious miles we had ridden together. She, too, was desperately in love, though she occasionally remembered her identity and that she was in the company of a badly shot-up young man and a broken-hearted cousin.

Most of the time, Diane and Foster rode on top of the stagecoach. When they did ride inside, their conduct was sweet to watch, yet it ignited fires of jealous rage and longing in me. It also seemed to have a remarkable effect on Gwen, who had been in a strange and somber mood since we started the journey. However, she gradually began to brighten and change more and more, perhaps divining something about Diane and Foster that escaped me. All of a sudden, she was transformed.

"Look here, if you people want to spoon, please get out on top," she said, surprising us all. If that wasn't the old Gwen Langdon, I didn't know who it was. Miss Barkley tried to appear offended, and Foster tried to look insulted, but they both failed.

The couple before me was undeniably happy. Despite the circumstances that could have made them serious and contemplative, they exuded youth and love. They were like magnets and steel, or powder and spark. I half-expected them to embrace right then and there, but instead, they settled for clasping hands. It was a moment that would stay with me forever - two people standing together on a ridge, embodying everything that was beautiful, passionate, and tragic. And I couldn't help but feel responsible for their happiness. I had been their undoing, but in the end, I was their salvation. It was a truth that I held close to my heart.

After Gwen's comment, Diane and Foster eventually made their way to the top of the stage. "Tim," Gwen whispered, "I think they're up to something. I heard a few words. I bet they're going to get married in San Antonio."

"It's about time," I replied. "But shouldn't they have told us?"

"Gwen, they've forgotten we exist."

"I'm just happy they're happy," Gwen said, and there was a long silence.

I was lying down, and Gwen took my hand without saying anything. My heart raced, but I didn't want to break the spell by opening my eyes or speaking. Eventually, Gwen spoke up. "Tim, I have to tell you something."

She hesitated, and I kept my eyes closed. "Have I been very sad?" she asked.

"You've been sad and strange, Gwen. It's worse than my bullet wounds," I replied.

She gripped my hand, and I felt her hair on my forehead and her breath on my cheek. "Tim, I swore I'd hate you if you-"

"I know," I interrupted. "Let's not talk about it."

"But I don't hate you," she said.

"I love you," I said, desperation creeping into my voice. "And I can't give you up!"

"But, Gwen, can you move on? Can you forget?" I asked, hoping against hope.

"Yes," she replied. "That terrible feeling has faded with every mile we've traveled. Little by little, mile after mile, it's gone! But I have to be honest with you, Tim. You never had any sense!"

At her words, my heart sank. But then she opened her arms, and we were reunited. It was a moment of pure joy, so overwhelming that it left me numb.

"Yes, Gwen," I said. "No man has ever had such a wonderful girl."

"Tim, I never took off your ring," she whispered.

"But you hid your hand from my sight," I replied quickly.

"Oh, Tim, we're as crazy as the lunatics outside. Let's think a little," she said.

I was happy to have no thoughts at all, just to feel her close to me. But then she asked, "Tim, will you give up the Ranger Service for me?"

"Indeed I will," I replied without hesitation.

"And leave Texas, never to return until the day of guns and Rangers and bad men and even-breaks is past?" she asked.

"Yes," I said firmly.

"Will you come with me to my old home? It was beautiful once, Tim, before it was let run to rack and ruin. A thousand acres. An old stone house. Great mossy oaks. A lake and river. There are bear, deer, panther, wild boars in the breaks. You can hunt. And ride! I have horses, Tim, such horses! They could run these scrubby broncos off their legs. Will you come?" she asked.

"I rather think I will," I said, excitement building in my chest. "But, dearest, after I'm well again, I must work. I've got to have a job."

"You're indeed a poor cowboy out of a job! Remember your deceit. Oh, Tim! Well, you'll have work, never fear," she said with a laugh.

"Gwen, is this old home of yours near the one Diane speaks of so much?" I asked.

"Indeed it is," she replied.

"My land has been well-maintained, while hers has been neglected. We'll have to work on fixing that," I said. "Agreed," she replied. "But there are formalities we need to take care of first." I looked at her, noticing a soft flush on her cheeks. "What do you mean?" "We need to make a formal agreement," she explained. "But before we do that, can you try to bring back the Gwen Langdon who used to torment me? The one who broke promises and leaned from his saddle? Kiss me, Gwen!" As we neared Uvalde, Gwen and I sat together, watching the sun set behind distant mountains. We were leaving the wild and barren border behind, and the memories of its haunting faces and wild life were slowly fading away. Other Rangers, with less to lose, would continue the work until the border was safe. The great state of Texas had a destiny to fulfill, and one day, the role of the Rangers in that destiny would be written in history.

THE END.

Printed in Dunstable, United Kingdom